Stealing South

A Story of the Underground Railroad

Also by Katherine Ayres

Family Tree

North by Night:
A Story of the Underground Railroad

Silver Dollar Girl

Stealing South

A Story of the
Underground Railroad

Katherine Ayres

Delacorte Press

Published by
Delacorte Press
an imprint of
Random House Children's Books
a division of Random House, Inc.
1540 Broadway
New York, New York 10036

Visit us on the Web! www.randomhouse.com/kids
Educators and librarians, for a variety of teaching tools, visit us at
www.randomhouse.com/teachers

Library of Congress Cataloging-in-Publication Data

Ayres, Katherine.
    Stealing South / by Katherine Ayres.
        p.   cm.
    Companion volume to: North by night.
    Summary: Sixteen-year-old Will Spencer leaves home to become a
peddler, but gets more than he bargained for when he agrees to go to
Kentucky, steal two slaves, and help them reach their brother in
Canada.
    ISBN 0-385-72912-X
    1. Underground railroad—Juvenile fiction. [1. Underground
railroad—Fiction. 2. Fugitive slaves—Fiction. 3. Peddlers and
peddling—Fiction. 4. Slavery—Fiction.] I. Title.
PZ7.A9856 St 2001
[Fic]—dc21   00-058974

The text of this book is set in 12.3-point Goudy.

Book design by Susan Dominguez

Manufactured in the United States of America

May 2001

10 9 8 7 6 5 4 3 2 1
BVG

For our travelers,
Bill and Susan

Chapter 1

. . . the Railroad's character was engraven, as by a pen of fire, in the hearts and consciences of men, burning deeper and deeper. . . .

H. U. Johnson
From Dixie to Canada

"Remember, Tom, if you hear horses, don't speed up, no matter what."

"I know, Will. You told me that at least five times on the last ride."

"The last ride was practice," I replied. "This one's for real. We have a passenger under the floorboards, so you've got to be careful."

We sat in Papa's wagon heading north from Atwater to Ravenna, a trip I'd made so often, I could have dropped the reins, for my horses knew the way. But this time my horses weren't doing the pulling and my hands weren't holding the reins. My younger brother, Tom, was making his first trip, and I was making my last in the dim light of a quarter moon.

"That Noah, he seemed pretty scared," Tom said, lowering his voice to a whisper.

"You'd be scared too, if you were all alone in a strange Northern place, getting hauled from hither to yon by folks you didn't know. He didn't look much older than you, Tom. Imagine that."

"No thanks. I'd just as soon stay put. Lucky for me, I can."

We were lucky, I thought, at least Tom was. He liked Atwater, Ohio. Loved the land and the life of a farmer. Course, him loving it was lucky for me as well, for it meant Papa could count on Tom for help in the fields and would allow me to leave. Tomorrow at first light I would begin my new life. But I had one last trip to make, and there wasn't a soul I'd rather be making it with than Tom. I'd been driving for the Railroad on dark nights like this one for years and was leaving my route to my brother.

As if reading my thoughts, he started in on me again, trying to talk me out of it. "You sure you really want to leave home? Think of Mama's cooking! A peddler's wagon can't be very comfortable, compared to our house. It's going to be mighty lonely with just your horses to talk to."

"My team's got more sense than most folks," I said. "A little peace and quiet will be a nice change from all the biddies of Atwater grinding our names in the mud."

Until three years ago, I'd liked our town and most of

the people in it. But that was before my sister Lucy got herself caught transporting a slave baby north to Canada and claimed she was the child's mother to save its life. After that, Lucy couldn't come back, and now half the town treated the rest of us Spencers like we'd caught the plague. Somehow, it didn't bother Tom like it did me. He was kind of a duck, and the whispers and rumors rolled right off his back like water. Me, I answered every snub and insult with my fists, and I'd gotten tired of it all.

"Will, the Reverend told me Noah's been chased on his trip north," Tom said, his voice still quiet. "He's heard hounds baying and had to wade the creeks several nights."

That made me sit up straight. "All the more reason for us to be careful, then. You got your excuses ready if somebody stops us."

"Who's going to believe some girl would want me to come calling?" Tom demanded. "Even if I liked the notion, which I don't."

"Give it a year or two," I said, grinning. "Girls ain't so bad. Might even find you like kissing."

Tom rolled his eyes. "You won't get me kissing some girl. Trading spit, that's all it is."

"Maybe. But how will you know unless you give it a try?" I'd kissed a couple of girls and liked it just fine, but I was sixteen, nearly grown. Tom was just coming up on thirteen and still had a lot to learn.

His elbow poked me hard in the ribs just as my ears caught the sound of distant hoofbeats. He tensed beside me and I listened carefully. Sounded like more than one horse, and the riders were coming from behind, the dangerous direction—somebody might be tracking Noah.

A sweat broke out on my forehead, and I rapped on the floor of the wagon, warning Noah to be extra quiet. I hoped he wouldn't panic. "Remember, Tom, don't speed up. Makes you look like you've got something to hide."

"You want to take the reins, Will? I don't mind if you do." Tom's voice shook.

My fingers itched to grab the reins, but if Tom was going to take on the route, he'd have to take on the trouble that sometimes came with it. I slapped him lightly on the shoulder. "You drive. You'll do just fine."

He gave me a quick nod and sat straighter, squaring his shoulders. It was my turn to poke him in the ribs. "Relax. Don't go all stiff and nervous. Think about kissing again."

He chuckled and shook his head. "You going to tell me the names of all the girls you've kissed, since you're such an expert?"

As the horses grew closer, I could hear the voices of dogs yapping and knew I had to keep Tom from tensing up again. "Your first lesson in kissing is not to shout the girl's name to the world. Not if you want to kiss her more than once." I paused, then whispered, "Dogs, you hear them?"

"Yep."

"You ready?"

"Nope. But I'll do what it takes."

That I could believe, for although I'd mostly been driving lately, before our sister Lucy got caught and the town grew suspicious, our family had run an underground Railroad station at our farm. Back then, Tom had helped plenty, even when he was pretty young.

The hoofbeats grew louder and closer, and the dogs set up a loud baying howl. Within minutes two strangers in dark clothing pulled even with us, one on each side of the wagon.

"Evening, gentlemen," I said, making my voice friendly and cheerful. "Hope you've got room to pass. Sorry if we're traveling too slow for you."

The man on my side answered in a gruff voice. "You could slow down and even stop, if you wouldn't mind. We'd like to talk to you."

"Sure thing," I replied. "Pull up there, Tom. Let's have a word with these fellas."

Tom pulled the team to a stop, and as he did, the two men reined in their horses and dismounted quickly. I swung down from the wagon and placed my body between them and the wagon bed. As soon as Tom had tied off the reins, he joined me. It was one of those times I blessed Papa's large size, for even though I wasn't all the way grown, I stood half a head taller than the men. I hoped that in the dark they wouldn't be able to tell how young Tom and I really were.

Around our feet three hounds circled, with loud,

excited barks. Tom knelt immediately and began talking to the dogs. "Hey there, fella. That's a boy. Good dog."

"Name's Chester, and this here's Robert. Who might you fellas be?"

"I'm Will and this is my brother, Tom," I said, carefully omitting our last name just in case they'd heard tales of the Spencer family and what wicked abolitionists we were. "We live around here, how about yourselves?"

"Just passing through. What brings you out on a dark summer's night?"

"Well, sir." I tried to make my voice sound nervous. Wasn't hard.

Tom had planted himself firmly next to me, between the men and what they were most likely looking for. "Truth is, my brother's riding out to spark a girl who lives up the road a piece," he said.

"Tom!"

"It's true. He's hoping she'll sneak out to meet him and drug me along to keep our folks from getting suspicious."

The men laughed.

Good job, Tom, I thought. "But I seem to remember that the gal I'm visiting has a younger sister you've been making calf eyes at for months. Unless I miss my guess, there'll be two gals climbing out a window tonight."

Tom looked down, then bent to scratch the ears of the dogs again. They'd calmed quite a bit and seemed more interested in sniffing Tom's boots than the wagon.

"You wouldn't mind if we looked into your wagon,

would you?" the second man asked. "Fact is, we're hunting for something that's gone missing."

"We didn't take nothing of yours," Tom said. "Only thing we've got in our wagon is a couple of straw bales."

There was an edge to my brother's voice, and it made me nervous. We couldn't let these men think we were hiding something. "Help yourself," I said loudly. "Look all you want. Mind you don't scratch yourself on the binding wire on those bales."

The men shoved up close to the back of the wagon and tossed the straw bales around some. All I could think of was poor Noah, right underneath the boards, hearing all that racket. If I were in his shoes, I'd be sweating a river.

Tom kept messing about with the dogs, which was a good thing, for our wagon appeared mostly empty if a person didn't know to search below the floorboards. The dogs were more dangerous to our passenger than all the snooping their owners might do; they could sniff out fear faster than a flea.

Under my breath I kept whispering to myself, "*Hurry up, just hurry up!*" Well, they didn't hurry, but they did quit looking after a while and remounted their horses. "A good evening to you, boys," the first man said. "Good luck with your young ladies."

"And good luck with your hunting," I said, as polite as Mama at an afternoon ladies' social, while in my heart I wished him the exact opposite.

Tom and I stood and watched the men ride out of sight

before we called to Noah that we were all safe, and climbed back into our wagon. Even then Tom didn't start up the road right away, but waited.

"You making sure they're really gone?" I asked him.

"I guess. Mostly I'm waiting for my heart to stop making such a racket in my chest."

"You did a good job, brother," I said. "Those dogs must have known how much you like tending critters. They couldn't get enough of you."

Tom grinned. "Wasn't me they liked, it was the bacon grease I smeared on my boots. I figured if we ran into any trouble and some dogs had me to smell, they might not be quite so interested in our friend Noah." And with that he clicked to the horses and we were off.

"That's a great trick. Wish I'd thought of it. Guess I don't have to worry about you anymore," I said. "Maybe girls will like the smell of bacon grease too, and you'll get some kisses after all."

Chapter 2

Truth be told, I wasn't expecting much more to happen that night, and the rest of the trip went smooth. With a dry road underfoot, the team made good time to Ravenna and the next station.

It wasn't until we were unloading our passenger from under the floorboards of the wagon that anything unusual happened. While Tom fed and watered the horses, I gave Noah a hand to pull him out, knowing he must be cramped and sore from the ten-mile ride.

As he stood in the dim light of the Quaker doctor's barn, he cleared his throat. "Mr. Will . . ."

Now that I could study him up close he looked about the same size as Tom, which meant he was only a couple of years younger than me. "Call me Will. I ain't no mister yet."

"Will, then," he went on. "That preacher man back at the church, he say you be travelling south. That true?"

"Yep. Got me a fine wagon and some money saved up from hauling goods for folks. I'm aiming to turn myself into a peddler. Do some trading and see the country awhile."

"What place? Where you going?"

It wasn't a secret, but I couldn't figure why he was asking. "Might start in Wheeling, get my supplies there. Then aim deeper into Virginia, Kentucky maybe. Why?"

The fella scuffed his toe in the dry dirt of the barn floor. "The preacher man, he say you a good friend to folks on the run."

"I do my best."

Tom had finished with the horses and stepped close to us. "Where are you heading with all these questions, Noah?"

He looked down like he was studying the floor. "I got troubles."

"What kind of troubles?" I asked.

"Family. Down Kentucky." His voice went soft and I had to strain my ears to hear him.

"Slaves?" Wherever there were slaves there was trouble, to my mind.

"Yep. A brother and sister. I be the first to run. I need a slave stealer for the rest."

10

"A slave stealer? What's that?" Sounded ominous in my ears. I glanced at my brother, but Tom just shrugged.

"Sorta like the catchers, only upside down. Ain't got much money, but I can pay you some now and more later if you bring him."

"I don't understand," Tom said. "What's a slave stealer do? Why are you talking about paying?"

"You goes down and steals slaves, right off the farm," Noah explained.

I stared at him, hard. "You mean from the master?" Whew, that would take some nerve.

"Uh-huh, right under his nose. Person got to pay somebody for that, Will. It be real dangerous."

"Hold on. I've been taking people north since I was eleven or twelve. I never once got paid or wanted to. Where are your brother and sister now? Where's the farm?"

"Will," Tom warned. "You can't be thinking—"

"Hush, Tom, let the fella talk."

Noah looked from me to Tom and back again. "Winchester. Ain't far from Lexington. Out the country. But I ain't got money enough for both. Just bring my brother up now. He the one in danger. I'll save for my sister later."

My cheeks burned and I could feel my temper simmer. "Look. I work the Railroad because I believe it in. Stop talking about paying." My voice rose to a shout, but I didn't care. "If you've got family in trouble, I might help, but I won't take your durn money."

Noah looked up from the floor and stared at one of the

barn stalls. Finally he reached into his shirt and drew out a necklace, a rawhide thong with a stone arrowhead threaded onto it, and placed it in my hands.

As I held it I ran my thumb over the stone's smooth surface, still warm from Noah's chest. Along each side, I could feel the notches where the flint had been flaked away and at one end, the sharp point. Arrowheads like this showed up in Ohio dirt, too, when we ran the plow through Papa's fields each spring. Tom and I had made quite a collection.

"You find these with your brother?" I asked, unable to keep myself from staring at my own brother's face and imagining him in deep trouble somewhere. From the look he gave me, I knew Tom was having the same thoughts.

"Yep. Me and James. My sister, Susannah, she shines them up for us. Will you go after him? Please? I'd go back myself but . . ."

"But you'd get caught, sure as the sun comes up," Tom said. "You can't be the one to go."

In the flickering lantern light I thought I saw dampness on Noah's cheek. It made my throat go dry. If I were Noah and my brother needed help . . .

"I got no map." Noah sniffed and continued. "But I can tell how I come north. You go back the same way, you sure to find James and Susannah. Tell them Noah sent you and show my arrowhead for proof. They do what you say."

I nodded. I knew about where Lexington, Kentucky, was, and I could surely find Winchester. With good directions and a little luck, I could hunt down the right farm, and one way or another, get Noah's family headed north. The thought of all that sneaking around set my head to spinning, but I'd never said no to a challenge yet. Shoot, not many fellas got the chance to show one of those slave owners what for, and I might enjoy that. It would mean making a few changes in my plans, though.

Some uncertainty must have showed on my face, for Noah shook his head sadly. "I know I be asking too much. You got no reason to take on my troubles. I'll just find a way to go get him myself." He reached for the arrowhead, but I glared and put the thing around my own neck.

"Dang it, I never said it was too much. Just needed to think it over. If I was to go down to Kentucky, where would I look for them?"

"I give you all that, but one thing. You got to hurry. James—he getting too old. He don't make free this summer, we never going to find him. Will you hurry?"

Tom didn't say anything, just wore a serious look and rubbed his knuckles along his jaw.

"All right. I'll go as fast as I can, but why? What will happen if I don't bring him out this summer?"

"Cotton. Them cotton fields just swallow him up." Noah explained it all in a soft, patient voice like a person might use to gentle horses. "You got to get him out now, Will. James be twelve. He nearly grown. You don't get him out soon, he gonna get his self sold down to Mississippi and we never find him again. Not until we all meet up in heaven."

At that word, *heaven*, my breath caught and I couldn't speak.

"How come people get sent farther south?" my brother asked in a quiet voice.

"Them cottonfields in Mississippi. Georgia. Need lots of folks to plant and hoe and pick."

"Why?" Tom continued. "Don't enough people already live in Mississippi and Georgia?"

Noah scowled. "Not hardly. They take anybody they can get. Besides, there be extra people in Kentucky and Virginia and Carolina. Master can make a good bit of money if he sell folks."

"What do you mean, extra people?" I didn't understand how people could be counted as extra.

Noah shrugged and looked at us for a while, like he was making up his mind about something. Then he started to speak, slowly and carefully. "It go like this. Some places the land be too hilly, or played out from growing tobacco. Instead of crop farming, folks there be farming us."

I couldn't figure what he was getting at. "What do you mean?"

"Breeding. Breeding slaves."

"For real?" Tom's voice came out in a whisper.

I couldn't wrap my mind around his words, they

sounded so wrong. Not horse or cattle breeding, but slaves. People!

"Master, he keep a bunch of women but only a few men. You don't need but a man or two for making babies. Sometimes, master, he do that job himself."

Some of this I'd heard before, but not from a person who'd really been there and seen it. Mostly, we didn't talk much with the folks we carried, for their safety and ours. "Then he sells the babies?"

Noah nodded, his face grim. "The men and the grown boys like me get sold down the river. Sold like plow horses instead of getting treated like folks."

"So you ran?" Tom asked.

"Yep. Got tall as a man. When we hear news of a soul driver at the next farm, buying up people I cut and run. No time to bring the rest of the family."

"And now James is in trouble, and you want me to hurry down there and find him." I shook my head and pondered it. Soul dealers, slave stealers, breeding—the words tasted so bad in my mouth, I wanted to spit. Tom and I had learned a peck of notions in just a few minutes. We'd gotten a real education.

Tom stepped back and readied the horses for our trip home as Noah and I talked awhile longer. He gave me clear directions and told me about an old man, a black-smith named Mister Ezekiel, who might help if I was having trouble finding the right farm. "I got a song for you to carry," he said. "You listen first, then sing with me."

"You don't want me singing," I warned. "I open my mouth, I sound like a cow in sore need of milking."

"Amen to that," my brother said, laughing.

"Can you whistle?"

"A bit."

He sang the song three times, and on the last time I did my best to whistle along. I tried to hang on to the words, too, for in my mind they fit together with that blacksmith. It was the story of Ezekiel and the wheel, from the Bible, set to a sprightly tune. And if I closed my eyes, I could see wheels spinning all right, the wheels of my wagon heading south to rescue James.

Once Noah had finished the singing lesson, Tom and I took him inside to hide in the Quaker doctor's attic. By the time we left, we had a plan. The very next night the doctor would point Noah in the direction of Windsor, Ontario, Canada, the final stop for many travelers on the Underground Railroad. Noah would wait there until I could send along James and Susannah.

As Tom and I rode back to Atwater that night I didn't say much, just stuck my hand inside my shirt and fingered the arrowhead Noah had given me. First time in my life I was wearing a necklace, but I couldn't think of a better place to keep it safe.

A person had taken care and polished the stone until the flint felt smooth. And I'd carry it back to Kentucky and find her. Made my heart thump to think on it—I was about to turn thief.

Chapter 3

Later, as we neared home, Tom finally broke our long silence. "You planning to tell Mama and Papa about Noah and this slave stealing?"

"Nope, and you'd better not tell them either. I'll just say I've changed my mind and decided to stock up in Cincinnati instead of Wheeling—see a bit of Ohio before going south. Mama's upset enough about me leaving home, no point making her fret more. And traveling as a peddler will be the perfect disguise for a slave stealer."

"I won't blab," Tom said.

He unhitched Papa's team and settled them into their

stalls while I checked on my own pair of gray geldings, Charlie and Sam. "You boys get a good rest now, so you'll be ready to travel in the morning." Sam nickered.

"You coming in, Will?" Tom asked.

"I doubt I'd sleep much. You go on. I've got some packing to do. I'll see you tomorrow."

"You sure? I could stay up. . . ."

"Go on. After all the excitement with the slave catchers and then Noah, I could use a little quiet."

"Me too."

Tom left and I busied myself with my own wagon. I'd hauled most of my belongings out to the barn earlier that day, so I could pack up the wagon with tools, spare clothes, and such by lantern light.

One small bundle made me stop and think—my cash supply. I'd saved up plenty from hiring out to neighboring farmers and hauling goods for them during the past three years, and Papa had given me a hefty sum, as an investment. If I folded all the money in a length of muslin, then tied it around my stomach like a corset, it ought to be safe enough. In Cincinnati I'd buy stock; then later Papa and I would split the profits.

I rechecked my list of merchandise. Mama and Papa had helped me figure what farm folk would want a traveling store to carry. Foolish things like ribbons and laces, serious things like salt and spades and hayforks.

Finally, when the wagon was ready, I reviewed Noah's directions in my mind. And I whistled that song about the wheel, just to be sure I hadn't forgotten it. I doubted

I'd need that blacksmith's help, but it didn't hurt to have a little something in reserve if things went wrong.

As the sky went from black to gray, I walked out of the barn and across Papa's fields, breathing in the damp smell of plowed earth and saying my goodbyes to the place. I bent and grabbed up a handful of dirt.

Tom loved the rich black soil, and it seemed right that he was staying here to help Papa. But farming wasn't the life for me, tied down in a single place all the time. Living with chores that regulated your days worse than any ticking clock. No, sir.

As I reached the edge of our farthest field a big old black crow flew overhead and cawed at me in his raspy voice. I took a deep breath and cawed right back at him, full to overflowing with the joy of a new day rising and a new road to travel.

"I'm flying, just like you are," I told that crow. "And I bet I'll see me some fine places, too."

When I returned from the fields, the family was awake and gathering for breakfast. Tom shoveled away his plateful of bacon and eggs, and I myself was plenty hungry, but Mama, Papa, and Miranda mostly picked. Then they marched with me out to the barn, where Tom and Papa helped me hitch up.

"You can come back, anytime. You'll always have a place here," Mama said. She swabbed at her eyes with the back of one sleeve.

"Aw, come on, Mama. Don't cry. You know I'll stop in to see you every time I get nearby. I just can't live here."

"I know, William."

But that didn't stop her from crying. She checked my boxes in the wagon and folded up all my clothes and blankets just so, to get me off to a good start. She had to know I'd be living rough with unironed shirts and trousers that carried miles of dust. But Mama was Mama, which meant I had to go out all spruced up.

After the horses were hitched and ready, Papa bent to examine my right front wheel. "Did you grease the axle real well, son?"

Durn, I knew that wagon better than he did. I bought and paid for it myself, the team too. But still Papa had to check my gear and fill my ears with advice like I was all of nine years old! Another good reason to leave home, I decided. My folks would never treat me like a man until I'd proved myself.

Then I caught sight of Mama's red eyes again and my temper just faded away. Mama and Papa had known their share of hard times, so if they needed to fuss over me for a few minutes this morning, I could put up with it.

"Hey, Will. You almost forgot." Tom hurried into the barn with Miranda following on his shirttails. He passed me a basket packed with food for my trip.

"You packed those socks I knitted, didn't you?" Miranda asked. Standing there with her hands on her hips, she looked like a half-pint version of Mama and Lucy. Heaven help us, fellas, but the females in our family were bossy.

"I packed the socks right on top, shorty. And Tom, you know I'd never forget to take Mama's good cooking along."

That was the wrong thing to say—it brought another flood of tears. All that fretting could smother a fella. When they finally waved me off, I breathed a sigh. The day was cool, the dirt road still damp with dew and morning fog. Doves serenaded me as I drove.

"Giddyup, boys, we're off!" As we headed south, I felt a loosening inside, a breaking free. For three years now I'd kept the best of me hidden. Since Lucy'd left, I hadn't felt right talking much about abolition or my work on the Railroad, for it worried Mama and Papa too much these days. And Tom and Miranda, well, they'd seemed too young. So Charlie and Sam had heard words that not another living soul might guess, and I could count on the two grays not to blab what they knew.

As we passed the houses and farms on the south side of Atwater, I heard horses behind me and turned to look, but the new canvas top on my wagon blocked my view. I'd just have to wait them out.

Didn't take long. Within minutes two riders pulled even with me. The Smith brothers. Durn and blast!

"What we got here?" the older one called out. "I thought the town decided to clear these roads, keep the trash from piling up."

The younger brother grinned at me. "Why, if it isn't that no-account, Will Spencer. You know the one. Specializes in giving black eyes and split lips. Got a harlot for a sister and quivering Quakers for friends. Wonder where good old William be headed now?"

The tone of his voice made me reach beneath the

wagon seat for the horsewhip, but as I bent to grab it, something wet hit my cheek. Spit!

I yanked out the whip and snapped it, aiming for the closest one's hat, but they had kicked up their horses and I only grazed him.

With a sharp twist of my wrist, the whip flew again, landing me leaves and branches from a nearby maple tree. A handful of jays rose in the air and scolded. Sam blew and tossed his head; Charlie nickered.

Flinging the whip down, I hauled up on the reins and slid to the ground, then walked carefully past Sam until I could throw an arm around each of my horses.

"Sorry, boys. Didn't mean to spook you. It's them." Up ahead, the Smith brothers were only smudges of dust on the horizon.

Once the team had calmed, I climbed back to the wagon seat and we drove off again. "Atwater. It's behind us at last. What do you think, Charlie? How about it, Sam?"

Sam didn't have much to say, but Charlie, good old Charlie, did. He lifted his tail and dropped a pile. I started to laugh. If that was what Charlie thought of that wagon rut of a town, he was one smart horse. I agreed with him a hundred percent.

Chapter 4

For six days I drove south with the sun beaming down on me and a light breeze blowing. While I kept my horses brushed and shining, a thick layer of road dust gathered on my skin and clothing, but that didn't rile me in the least. In fact, I considered it a sign of being my own fella that for once in my life nobody could tell me to go scrub.

Then Old Man Weather blew some thunderheads my way and let them rip loose with torrent after torrent. That rain turned me and my dust into mud, and the road into ruts and bumps. When I wasn't sliding, I'd get a wheel stuck nearly to the axle.

That rain kept up all the way to Cincinnati, and by the

time I reached the edge of town, I needed a stable, for the horses had plowed through heavy muck and were tired. The rain hadn't stopped, but I was so wet a little more didn't matter, so I climbed down from the wagon seat and walked alongside, encouraging the boys. "Gee up there, Charlie. Keep on coming, Sam. We're in town now, can't be too much farther to the warehouse district by the river."

On a nice day, I might have noticed the summer green on the hills, but in the wet and mud all I had time to pay attention to was how steep the roads were, and how slick. I wasn't the only fella having trouble, for as I neared a crossroads I saw another wagon stopped and tilted with one wheel in a ditch.

"Need a hand there?" I called to the driver.

"I'd be obliged," he replied. "I've unloaded most of my supplies. So if you could help me push . . ."

"Sure thing." I led my team around the fella's wagon and secured them to a tree some distance ahead, so they wouldn't get spooked when the other team started to move. Then I returned and set my shoulder to the back of his wagon. His horses started in pulling, and I shoved from behind until I heard that sucking sound that means the mud has lost its grip. Of course, plenty of that old mud splashed up on me, adding to my own collection.

"Thank you there, young man," the other driver said. "I'm lucky a big strapping feller like you happened by. Anything I can do to return the favor?"

"I need a good cheap place to stay for a while, down

close to the river. Got any ideas?" I helped him reload his sacks of grain.

"Fox's Tavern," he said, pointing. "Straight ahead on this road for another half mile. Tell them Matthew Mason sent you and they're to treat you right." He tipped his hat to me, climbed back up to his seat, and urged his horses forward.

I made Fox's Tavern without further trouble, and after tending the horses, I was mighty glad to step into a copper tub and soak away the grime. Even better, while I was soaking, the sun decided to poke his face in my direction and some of the gray outside my window gave way to blue sky.

The tavern keeper gave me a small, clean room, and as I put on dry clothes I checked myself in the mirror above the dresser. My red hair stuck out every which way, making me look about as ferocious as one of those old-time Viking men Papa used to read about of a winter evening. If I didn't want to scare people to death, I'd better find a laundry *and* a barber.

It was while I sat in the barber's chair, listening to the snip of scissors and smelling bay rum hair tonic, that I got my first dose of southern Ohio.

"Ought to be strung up. That's a fact," said the man in the chair to my right. "Them Quakers are up to no good, what with their high-minded, uppity talk and their abolitionist foolishness. I'd be proud to offer 'em a rope for the hanging."

Such talk was common enough, from the Smith brothers and other simpleminded louts. And back home when I heard it, the speaker was always sorry afterward. I straightened, ready to plow the man's face with my fist, when the cold steel of the barber's scissors poked my neck.

"Easy there, young feller. Cain't hardly cut your hair straight if you're going to twitch."

"Hurry it up, then, I'm getting tired of this." I still wanted to plaster that man. Could have done it too. He was a runty little squirrel, skinny and droopy-looking. Scissors snipped near my ear, reminding me that I was a stranger here. I let out a sigh and hid my balled-up hands under the barber's cloth that draped my lap and shoulders.

The man on my left took up the conversation with a nod. "Right about that, Hiram. Them broad-brimmed hats is a sign of trouble, sure as Sunday. And they don't even call it Sunday. Biggest bunch of foolishness I ever heard. Imagine setting in church with nobody saying nothing. Jest waiting around for the Lord to strike you with lightning or some such. A man got to have his sins preached out of him. Fire and brimstone—that's God's way."

Hiram, the old squirrel, snorted and chimed back in. "Ain't it the truth? Why, if I had to sit still and quiet every Sunday morning, I wouldn't need no afternoon nap. I'd get all my sleeping done on God's time." He laughed, and it was an ugly sound.

"You done yet?" I asked the barber.

He brushed my hair back from my face and dusted off my neck. "You ain't shaving, young feller, so I won't charge you the full price."

"Thanks." Sliding from the chair, I flipped him a coin and practically ran out of that barbershop, slamming the door behind me. I was a Presbyterian, not a Quaker, but my Quaker friends from the Railroad were some of the best people around, people you could count on any time of day or night. How dare those men say such hateful things in public? Up in Atwater, when folks had meanness on their mind, at least they had the good sense to spout their venom in private, not shout it to strangers.

In a shop window, I peered at my reflection and checked the barber's work. My head was presentable, but the scowl on my face made me look ferocious. I took a deep breath and forced my mouth to relax.

Durn it, I'd hoped to leave all the fools behind in Atwater, but Cincinnati was worse. I kicked at a stone in the street, sending it all the way to the corner.

On the way back to the tavern, I thought hard and realized I'd have to keep a strong latch on my mouth until after I'd gotten to Kentucky and yanked James and Susannah free of that farm. Otherwise my temper would grab hold of me and betray my abolitionist beliefs to strangers. Southern strangers. Unless I spotted a man wearing one of those broad-brimmed Quaker hats, I'd have to keep my opinions to myself and talk only about trading goods or the weather. And I'd have to keep my fists in my pockets.

I scuffed along the street, but as the sun warmed my back, some of the ugliness fell away. Cincinnati was a mean place, but I didn't have to stay here. A traveling fella like me, I could stock my wagon and move on. Good riddance. With that thought, I stepped a little lighter.

A little boy walked up the street with his mama. He grinned and waved. The first real smile of the day spread across my face, and I wet my lips and started to whistle.

Papa had told me not to go to the shops to buy my goods, but to purchase in quantity at the warehouses. Time enough for that tomorrow, but as I walked I let my eyes wander over the goods displayed in the windows of the stores. Couple of places I actually walked right into, to get a better idea of what kind of ladies' frippery might sell well. I examined ready-made dresses, to see what color the cloth was, so I'd know what to buy.

A girl came over to me as I studied a row of straw hats. She had friendly dark brown eyes, and when she smiled, I smiled back. "You would like to buy a hat for someone? Your mother? Or your sister?"

"Um. Um. No. I'm not buying, I'm selling." My face heated up and I nearly ran from the store. I'd mumbled like a fool, and my face had probably turned as red as my hair.

She kept talking to me anyway. "You sell hats? Really?"

I knew how to talk to girls—I wasn't a dolt, just a little out of practice. I took a deep breath.

"I've got a wagon. Heading south to sell goods, back-country where there aren't too many stores," I explained. "I wanted some ideas about what ladies might buy. Nothing as fancy as this, of course."

"You are a businessman. You have come to the right

28

place. People say my family owns the nicest shops in Cincinnati." She nodded proudly.

"I'll be selling to country people, not city folks. But maybe you could show me which colors the women like best."

"Rose, lilac, blue, green. Pretty colors, but dark enough so they will not show a little dirt."

"Sounds good for country people," I said, as if I'd ever bothered to notice what colors of dresses country women wore.

"You will want black, too," she went on. "For mourning clothes."

This girl wasn't only pretty, with her dark wavy hair and shining brown eyes, she was smart, too. I was content to let her talk on, enjoying the slightly foreign sound of her voice.

"Now we are in July, so most people will have made their summer clothing already. You will want to carry winter cloth. How far south will you travel? It does not get so cold there."

I nodded and we talked on for five minutes or so, and it was the pleasantest time I'd spent since leaving home. Papa had warned me before I left Atwater. "There are fools everywhere, boy. Can't escape them, got to learn to deal with them."

If I hadn't believed Papa before, the trip to the barbershop had convinced me. But there were nice people everywhere too, helpful, friendly ones, if a person took the time to find them.

Chapter 5

The heavy, damp air of the riverfront and the noise of men unloading cargo greeted me the next morning at the warehouses. I hurried from place to place, trying to find the merchants with the best prices before the sun rose too high and stifled me.

I picked out combs and buttons, shoelaces, pins, needles, and threads from one warehouse. Nearby, a German cloth merchant gave me a good price on rolls of wool and muslin and calico, and offered to buy any skins or furs I might take in trade. He sent me to his brother-in-law, who sold home goods, and that man sent me on to a cousin who sold tools, so after four or five stops I'd ordered enough to stock my wagon to the top and arranged to pick it up in a day or two. Couldn't help feeling a bit worried about spending all that money so fast, but I'd bargained well and still had money left as Papa had advised so I could afford to splurge a little.

I owed everybody letters anyway; surely they'd welcome a present as well. I returned to the cloth merchant and picked out a few bright-colored hair ribbons for Miranda, then talked the man out of a nice length of brown velvet that would make Mama a new winter church dress. I felt more grown than ever before, a road traveler sending gifts home.

The sun climbed high, and my stomach was growling for a meal. The day before, I'd seen a café near the fancy shop where I'd talked to the pretty girl, so I wandered off in that direction. When I reached the café, lace curtains at the windows nearly scared me off, but I squared my shoulders, strode across the cobbled street, and opened the shop door before I lost my nerve. There she stood, the girl with the dark brown eyes, arranging a line of gloves on the wooden counter.

"Hello. It's me again. I came yesterday. . . ."

"Need more advice?" she asked with a smile. "Hats or gloves?"

"Um, not really. I just wanted a meal." I stared at the floor.

"There is a café across the street." She pointed toward the door. "Good food, or so they say." She fiddled with the fingers of a glove, making sure they were spaced just so.

31

What a fool I was, standing there trying to look interested in white net gloves. I took a deep breath and pushed out some words, hoping they made sense. "Um, I wanted you to come to dinner with me. My name's Will Spencer and I'm from the northern part of Ohio. I wanted to thank you for your help yesterday. Will you come to eat with me?"

She lifted her face toward me and smiled again. "I would like to, very much. I must ask Mama. You will have to meet her. Do you mind?"

What had I gotten myself into? I should have grabbed a quick plate at one of the catfish shacks on the riverfront.

"I'd be pleased to meet your mother." I grinned wide to hide the lie.

Two minutes later I shook hands with a tall, sturdy-looking woman with dark hair pulled back into a roll on her neck. "You vish to take Elise to the café?"

Elise. Her name was Elise. It was as pretty as she was.

"Yes, ma'am. She helped me yesterday and I wanted to say thanks."

"Ve eat our dinners in the shop."

"Mama, please. I've never been to the café."

"Ve eat our dinners in the shop," she repeated, her voice stern and unyielding.

"Please, ma'am. You can watch out the window. I'll walk her right across the street, real proper. I just wanted to thank her for her help. My mother raised me to treat girls polite. I've got sisters." I mumbled and blushed like a fool.

At last she nodded, then checked her watch and turned to Elise. "Vun hour. You vill be back to verk by vun-fifteen. And sit in the vindow vere I can see you!"

"We will," Elise promised. "Thank you, Mama."

Once out the door, she turned to me, her cheeks red. "Thank you, Will. Mama is very strict. No ruffians!"

"That's smart of her." I tried not to think what she'd call me if she knew how many eyes I'd blackened these last three years.

We found seats at a small round table and ordered up our meal, including lemonades.

"You haven't eaten here before?" It was a foolish thing to ask, but I couldn't find anything better.

"They only opened last month. Mama and I take our midday meal at the shop. Between customers."

"Do you and your mother run the store alone? Seems like a big place."

"We do work hard, but I like selling such nice clothes. Nice ladies, too, most of our customers. My uncle Frederick owns the shop. He owns many shops now, but he set this one up special so Mama and I could be independent. We live above the store."

She kept talking about her uncle, and how he'd started out like me, as a peddler. I couldn't help wondering where her father fit into all this, but I didn't know how to ask without poking my nose where it didn't belong. Instead I told her about my family, about Mama and Papa, Thomas and Miranda at home, and about Lucy, who studied at Oberlin College and spent her summers in Canada.

33

"A big family, so lucky. I just have Mama. Papa died before I was born. And my cousins, my uncle's children, are all old, married with babies. We have family back in Germany, too, but I don't remember them. We traveled here to make a new life when I was very young."

I didn't know what to say to all that. I could hardly tell her the real reasons I'd left Atwater behind—that the town and most everybody in it thought I was a bully and scorned my family for Lucy's supposed sins. So I just let her talk on, enjoying the touch of Germany I heard in her voice and the way her dark hair waved around her face.

"Canada sounds so exciting. Except for Germany, I have lived only in Ohio. Mostly in Cincinnati. And I hear Canada is cool. A day like this, I would like a cool place."

She pushed the heavy weight of her hair off her neck and I felt my cheeks burn.

"More lemonade?" I offered her. I sure needed some.

"Yes. Please."

We'd finished our meal by the time the town clock chimed one o'clock. I paid for our food and walked Elise across the street. She wasn't due back just yet, but I couldn't think of an excuse to keep her outside in the noonday heat. Inside the shop my eyes lit on the row of gloves she'd been fiddling with earlier. There. A real reason to keep talking to her.

"How much do you charge for those gloves?" I asked. "I might send a packet to my sister up in Canada. She's staying in a real small town. No nice shops."

Elise showed me two kinds of gloves, as if I could really

34

notice the difference. All I could see was how slender her fingers were and how her nails were round and smooth from buffing.

"Pick the ones you like best," I decided. "Lucy will like them too."

"Shall I wrap them and send them on for you? We have brown paper and string for packages."

"I owe her a letter. So, I'll make up the packet myself. But I wouldn't mind the offer of paper and string. And if you could direct me to the post office." Anything to keep me in that store an extra minute.

Elise gave me directions as I counted out the money for the gloves. She bustled around with paper and string and even found a small box. "Canada is a long way. You will want your package to get there safely."

"Thanks." I wanted to say something else, but wasn't sure how. This girl turned me into a dolt, unable to spit out real sentences. As she handed me the package, I just blurted it out: "I leave tomorrow. For Kentucky. I could be gone awhile. I'd like to think . . ." My voice gave out, or my courage—I don't know which.

"Yes?"

"I'd like to visit you again when I've sold my goods. I'll need to come back to Cincinnati to restock. I'd like to . . . to take you to supper when I get back. Would you be willing?"

It seemed like I held my breath forever.

She finally nodded and smiled. "I would like to have supper with you, Will Spencer. When you come back."

It was all I could do to get out of that shop and shut the door before I raced down the street and let out a yell.

I had a wagon ready to head south, a new life spread out before me like a landscape picture, and an adventure planned with Noah's family to keep things exciting. Now I had a girl waiting for me when I came back. What could possibly go wrong?

Chapter 6

The first wrong thing showed up not ten minutes after I left Elise and her family's shop behind. A flag fluttered out in front of the post office and a knot of men milled close to the building next door to it. I slipped into the crowd and sniffed around to discover what they were up to.

The building was built of red brick and sat on the corner, so one brick wall faced the street. That wall seemed to hold the men's interest. As I edged in closer I could see what looked like handbills pasted up onto the bricks. One man stood at the center of the crowd, with rolls of paper under one arm and a bucket of glue, sticking new papers up with a brush.

Men studied the papers and called to each other: "This here's a live one," or "How about that, Buster? Three hundred dollars for a pair!"

Lucky for me I was tall and could look over the heads of some of the fellas in the front, but what I saw made my stomach turn sour.

ONE HUNDRED DOLLARS REWARD

RAN AWAY FROM THE UNDERSIGNED ON THE 10TH OF JUNE, A MULATTO FELLOW BY THE NAME OF ROMAN, ABOUT THIRTY YEARS OLD, LARGE WHISKERS, 5 FEET 9 OR 10 INCHES HIGH, WELL MADE, AND WEIGHS PROBABLY ABOUT 165 LBS. HE IS CRIPPLED IN HIS LEFT HAND, AND LIMPS SOME ON HIS RIGHT LEG WHEN HE WALKS. ANY PERSON WHO WILL APPREHEND SAID FELLOW, AND DELIVER HIM TO ME, OR SECURE HIM IN ANY JAIL SO THAT I GET HIM AGAIN, SHALL RECEIVE THE ABOVE REWARD.

MAY 24, 1854
JOSEPH DAVIS,
LEXINGTON, KENTUCKY

I scanned the wall and my heart drummed a funeral march in my chest—*Simon. Tom. George. Hannah. Lizzie. Peter.*

There had to be at least fifty of those handbills posted, some fresh and white, others tattered, yellowed, and spotted with rain. It was a wall of misery. Every handbill meant at least one slave had run and was being chased. And the men reading seemed excited, like they were having a party or something.

"Wouldn't mind finding that gal," one man said, pointing. He grinned, spat, and his tobacco-stained teeth showed ugly and brown. "Them young ones know how to show a feller a good time."

"You find her, Samuel, share her around a little 'fore you send her on down for the reward."

"Might just do that," tobacco-teeth Samuel replied.

The afternoon sun scorched the back of my neck and all of a sudden my hands stung. I looked down—my fists were balled so tight, my nails had cut deep lines into my palms. I wasn't sure whether I'd lose my meal or my temper first, so I pushed my way out of the crowd and looked for a quiet place to stand and catch a breath.

Around the corner, a shaded alleyway ran between two rows of buildings. I took deep, heaving breaths and stretched out my fingers. Sure, I'd heard about runaway notices before, but I'd never seen one, let alone fifty. As far north as Atwater, Ohio, even folks who thought slavery was lawful weren't likely to go posting such wickedness up on a public wall. But Cincinnati was just one short river crossing away from slave territory and all the wretchedness that came along with it.

My stomach still felt sour, but it settled enough that I wasn't likely to spew on the street. I wanted to go back and tear down those handbills, but there was only one of me and twenty or more of those men. If I stepped back into that crowd, I wouldn't be able to control my temper. Just the memory of that man Samuel and his filthy talk about some runaway girl made me smack the stone backside of a building a good one. My palm got scraped and bled a little, but it was worth it.

From the alleyway I meandered around the next street, taking the long way to the post office. That's where the next wrong thing happened. Sure enough, there were letters waiting for me. One from Lucy and one from Mama. They looked like they'd been chewed by a big dog on their way to Cincinnati. If it had been just one messy letter, I might not have paid attention, but as I started to lift the flap on Mama's envelope, it felt like the glue wasn't stuck down too well. I checked Lucy's—sure enough, that flap was loose too. It made me feel all crawly, like a snake was twitching up my backbone.

I stomped up to the man who stood behind the counter and stuck the letters under his nose. "Look here, mister. Somebody went and opened my letters. That ain't right."

"Watch what you say, young feller. You wouldn't want to tell me my business now, would you? You being a stranger and all?"

"It still ain't right," I hollered, taking a step closer to the man. Out of the corner of my eye, I saw two other men move alongside. They glared.

I grabbed my letters and walked sideways out of that place, not daring to turn my back on those men. Jamming my letters into my trousers pocket, I strode away toward the tavern, stopping a couple of times to look over my shoulder and see if someone followed. I didn't see anybody but couldn't shake off that crawly feeling till I'd lumbered up the tavern stairs and bolted the door tight.

Cincinnati was a durned rotten place where they posted handbills on a public wall for slave catchers to drool over and opened a person's private mail as if they had a right to it. If I hadn't known better, I'd have thought I'd already crossed the Ohio River and entered one of the slave states. But no, this was Ohio, my home state. Free soil, and an abolitionist hotbed, according to Papa.

I shook my head and shame washed over me. Shame and something else. The hairs on the back of my neck bristled, and I realized that my coming journey promised more than adventure. Those ugly men and the handbills they were reading were a threat, not just to the runaways, but to me once I started snooping around for Noah's family.

A cold lump of fear settled into the pit of my stomach, and it would take a heap of miles between this place and me before I could dislodge it.

Chapter 7

June 5, 1854

Dear William,

Cincinnati must be quite the place, filled with fine shops. How I'd like to travel there one day. Perhaps you will find time to take me and show me the sights.

Your father and Thomas spend long days in the fields. We made our first hay cutting, and it was abundant, for we've had fine rains so far. The Lord certainly takes care of our needs, as the Book says, even before we ask.

I've prayed for patience and guidance with Miranda. Some days I've been sorely tempted to duck that child into the washtub and scrub away her crotchety disposition. She's not been herself since you left. And last night

I received an answer of sorts and began to understand why she's been so sulky.

Thomas had spent a long week clearing land, and when Saturday afternoon came, he went off to the swimming hole with a mob of boys. When he returned home, Miranda lit into him like a mother cat, claws out and hissing. It seems she thinks you and Lucy have left her. Not that you left to begin your own lives, but that you specifically left her behind.

When Thomas went off swimming, she thought he meant to leave her behind as well and was sneaking away. She made him vow not to go off when he turned sixteen. For Thomas that was an easy vow to make, so our youngest has regained some of her cheery disposition. As I think on this, if perhaps you have the chance to show me Cincinnati, you will show it to Miranda as well and this will restore you to her good graces.

But aside from Miranda's spell, we are all in good health and content. We pray for your sister Lucy, as she ministers to the folk in Canada and for your safety and good fortune as you load your wagon and travel the back trails. Write soon with your news.

With love,
Mother

That last part, about Lucy, stopped me. I could guess what some of the people around this town might think of my sister's work and worried whether Mama had given away anything. The words looked innocent enough, and

Lucy was far away from this durned river town, safe in a whole different country for the summer. Still, I hated that somebody had read the words Mama had meant for me. It spoiled the good feeling letters from home were supposed to give.

The Miranda parts made me laugh, though. What a little spitfire. Good thing I'd picked out a few ribbons to send her. She might forgive my desertion. But I'd no more bring Mama to this wicked town than fly to the moon and beyond. Mama was a good person. And little Miranda! Just walking through these cruel streets would spoil her. I wasn't about to let my baby sister find out how vile people could be. On the other hand, if she was as mad as it sounded, maybe she'd give these folk in southern Ohio what for!

I reached into the envelope for Lucy's note. This too had been read, and I hoped real hard that Lucy had been careful.

June 1, 1854

Dear Will,

How goes the trip? Mama wrote to say you'd changed plans somewhat, so I'm hurrying to write you in the hopes that the letter will arrive in Cincinnati before you do.

I am well settled and find Windsor a welcome respite from the heat. The lake is so near to this farm that breezes bless us every day, and at night, we often need a quilt. From what I hear, Cincinnati is sultry—the river only adds to the misery instead of freshening the land. Hope you find the Kentucky hills catch a few breezes as you travel south.

My summer work goes well. I teach reading, writing, and sums as usual. But because of the new year-round school here, the young people have made much progress since last summer. I've broken my students into two classes, one for beginners and one more advanced. Imagine having grandmothers and little ones in the same beginner's class. It challenges me, but I love it.

Every day I think of your travels. Go carefully, Will. And as you journey, I hope you'll keep up with your own studies of the natural world. In particular, traveling south, you'll have the opportunity to observe the wintering grounds for some of the wild Canada geese we've watched on their northward migrations. I've studied a bit with an ornithologist at the college, and I'll pass you his advice.

Approach these wintering grounds silently and with caution. I'm sure you will learn much that may prove both interesting and useful. You might also wish to study alternative paths for the fall migrations, as we in our part of Ohio only knew a few routes. Certainly there are Friends of Nature who might offer you such information.

Sorry to nag at you so, but as I'm turning into a teacher, I feel obliged to encourage your studies. Older sisters have such rights, you know, in spite of the fact that you've grown into a great lump of a boy. Truly,

Will, take care of yourself. Your wagon is solid built, and so are you. God bless you.

Fondly,

Lucinda

I reread the last half of Lucy's letter with relief. She was so smart. She'd used the code our family had long ago devised to speak of the runaways. It was as if she'd suspected that someone might nose into her letter, so she'd referred to the slaves as wild Canada geese. Their wintering grounds were the Southern farms and plantations. And I was to proceed carefully and silently. Made me wonder if Lucy suspected that my change of plans had a serious meaning. In any case, I would be careful as I searched for James and Susannah. Even yesterday I might have laughed off her cautions, but not today.

And the notion of alternative routes was a good one. My plan hadn't changed; I still hoped to carry Noah's family north in my wagon, but if troubles came, we should have options. Who better to help me discover those than the Quakers? Friends of Nature, Lucy had called them. Friends.

I wrote back to Mama and Papa and sent Miranda her own letter, with ribbons tucked inside. Made quite a packet, what with the cloth for Mama and a new penknife each for Papa and Tom.

Then I wrote to Lucy and told her about my mission in the same code she'd used. My words didn't sound very scholarly, but I threw in a few extra-fancy words like *migrations* and *wildlife habitations* and hoped anybody who wanted to snoop would think we were a family of owlish students.

It wasn't until I was ready to wrap and tie Lucy's bundle together that I found the biggest surprise of the day. Inside the box with the brown paper, the lace gloves, and the string, Elise had included a note. And nobody had messed with this one. It was all for me—a few lines of neat, curling letters—

> *Will Spencer, if you have the time and the inclination, I would be delighted to hear news of your travels. Send to: Elise Schmidt, Schmidt's Fine Ladies' Mercantile, Market Street, Cincinnati. If you name a post office, I will write back.*
>
> > *Your friend,*
> > *Elise*

I read it over and over, and itched to rush right to her shop and see her again.

If I had the time and inclination! Hallelujah! What a day! I'd found one friend in the rough and unwelcoming town of Cincinnati, and if I could just find a Quaker Friend before leaving, I'd be all right.

Chapter 8

Mama always says trouble comes in threes. I wasn't inclined to believe her, but Cincinnati did make me wonder. After that ugly wall of notices and having my mail opened, a little caution wouldn't hurt. That third bad thing might be waiting for me around any corner.

I needed to mail my packets and ask the postmaster to send on new mail to Winchester, Kentucky, but I couldn't inquire about any Quaker settlements at the post office, not after yesterday. I asked at the tavern instead and tried to sound rough.

"Got me some Bibles to deliver," I told the tavern keeper over supper, making up the story as I told it. "I'm supposed to find some of them Round-hat Quaker folks, not too far from Cincinnati. You know about any Quaker towns nearby?" I dug into my pork chops and sauerkraut, hoping that Quakers used Bibles, or if they didn't, that the tavern keeper didn't know about it.

"Some of them scattered here and yon," the man said. "Can't trust them a minute, I hear. You'd best get your money afore you unpack them Bibles."

"Scattered, you say?"

"Yep. Biggest batch would be up at Walnut Hills. About six miles north. Pretty enough town, if you don't mind odd praying and such." He wiped his hand on his apron. "You suppose they quiver and quake like the name says? Sounds like quite a show. Wouldn't mind seeing that."

Unable to think of a reply, I shrugged and stuffed another hunk of pork into my mouth. He'd given me a location; I should be grateful.

"And young man," the tavern keeper went on. "If you're going into them Ken-tuck hills, how about you bring me back a little white fire, if you get the chance? I'd make it worth your while."

"White fire?"

"Corn liquor. Home-cooked. Strong stuff they brew up in them hills. You trade some of your goods for the liquor, I'll pay you in cash money once you bring it back here. Some of them country folks don't have a cent, but they got plenty worth trading. Well?"

Durn, I'd talked like a rough traveling man, and now he was treating me like one. I couldn't turn the fella down

49

without looking like a fool, or worse, making him suspicious. Mama would skin me alive for trading spirits, but Mama wasn't here. "Guess I could haul corn liquor for you, if anybody offers me some." We shook hands on the bargain, and I tried to smile, but the grin felt pasted on.

Next morning, I got an early start and borrowed a riding horse from the stable. The tavern man was right; Walnut Hills was a pretty town, with wide lawns and tall black walnut trees. I figured I'd skipped Mama's prediction of triple trouble when I passed a big white house and saw the familiar outline of a Quaker hat, worn by an older man who was tending his garden.

At the gate I called in to him. "Friend, I've come to ask a favor. Could I please speak with you for a moment?"

He smiled, strode to the gate, opened it, and let me in. He led me to the front porch, which felt cool and shady after my morning ride. "How may I help thee?"

As I studied his sharp jaw and creased face, I was glad I'd planned my words carefully. He didn't look like the sort of man anyone should tangle with.

"I need a special kind of help." My throat felt thick and I cleared it. "I have a wagon which I've used to transport goods—very unusual goods—up in northern Ohio. I don't know the roadways too well in your part of the state, nor in Kentucky, where I'm headed. Have any advice?"

He smiled at me, but only with his mouth. His eyes kept a closed, stern look about them. "If thee wants roadways, why not ask a teamster?"

"I'm not looking for regular routes. I need special ones. Safe."

"Surely all God's people hope for safety," he replied, wearing that same thin smile.

All my planned speeches were worthless, so I sighed and spoke plainly. "Please, sir. These are hard times. I've hauled folks north toward Canada for four years now since the durned Congress passed that Fugitive Slave Act. I'm headed down to Kentucky to find a boy's brother before he gets sold south to the cotton fields. I'll need a safe route to come back in case we hit trouble."

"Why ask me about Kentucky? I'm an Ohio man."

I gripped the porch rail. He spoke politely, but he had no intention of answering my questions. I could hardly blame him. For all he could tell, I might be a catcher spying out routes, instead of a slave stealer, going on a rescue. Somehow or another I'd have to prove myself.

I thought about our work, our night trips. Maybe they used the same signals here. I reached out and rapped my knuckles on the porch rail, twice, then again. "Who's there?" After a pause I replied to my own question like a fool—"A Friend with a friend."

That at least brought a smile which encouraged me. Maybe he'd know some of the same people I knew. "In Atwater, Ohio. Salem, Ohio. I know the Strong families, Friends, all of them. They built my wagon. We've worked together. Perhaps you've heard of them."

"Perhaps," he said.

"There's Levi Strong and Amos," I continued. "The

ones I know best are Amos's family, Jeremiah and his sister, Charity. They're a little older than me. We all
worked together on a rescue three years ago. Maybe you
heard about it. We got caught, or my sister did. Jeremiah
and I took nine people out safe to Windsor, but my sister
Lucy got caught when she carried a baby north. Had to
leave town."

"Indeed?"

He was so stubborn, and I was running out of things to
tell. I took a deep breath and tried once more.

"My sister, Lucy Spencer. She's in Canada right now.
Summers, she teaches people reading and writing. During
the school year she attends the college at Oberlin. Jeremiah and Charity Strong, they went off to the Quaker
college at Swarthmore, Pennsylvania. People got suspicious, so they all had to leave town. Please, sir. I don't
know my way here."

As I spoke, a lonesome feeling swept over me. Lucy,
Jeremiah, Charity, and now me. We'd scattered, hither
and yon, strangers cast out into a world that could be
hard and cold, a world where caution came first and nobody trusted you.

At last the Quaker held out his hand to me in greet-
ing. "I am Benjamin Coleman. Thy name is?"

"Will. William Spencer." I shook his hand, hoping
he'd help me and that this wouldn't be my third dose of
trouble.

Chapter 9

That night I went to bed with my stomach full but my mind still unsettled. The old Quaker had been more than polite; he'd invited me to share a meal, and a hearty meal it was. But he'd been frugal with his words.

He'd told me which ferry to take across the river—at the first one, the ferryman overcharged strangers, so I should wait for the second. And there were two roads to Winchester, one busy and one less traveled. It was a start, but I could have learned that much from most any traveler. With the Quaker, though, I had less worry that someone might suspect me of mischief, or remember my red hair and report me if something went wrong. It was thin comfort.

At least my journey had a starting place and a full wagon, for after visiting with the Quaker man, I'd returned to the warehouses and loaded up my goods, giving me an early start on the morning. After working hard that day, and traveling some, I'd earned a good rest, but still couldn't sleep. The night air was humid and I tossed in the bed. Something still gnawed at my belly. What was it?

I closed my eyes and concentrated. That danged wall! Once I saw it again in my mind, I couldn't help myself. I had to go back.

Thick clouds hung in the night sky outside my window, covering up the stars and the moon's light, so I figured I could make my way without being seen. I grabbed a handful of sulfur matches and a candle stub from the dresser and shoved them into my trousers pocket, then crept down the tavern steps.

Outdoors, the night air felt heavy and dank, like the breath of a big dog when he pants on your face. I slipped along the streets in the shadows. When footsteps sounded, I ducked into the nearest alleyway and froze until the street grew quiet again. Three times that happened before I found the right street.

By night the wall of notices gleamed pale gray, bleached like old bones. I looked around. Nobody in sight. I struck a match and held my candle close. Even with the candle, the names were hard to make out, written real small like names didn't matter much. But the big words sure showed up—STOP THE RUNAWAY! $200

54

REWARD! RAN! FIVE HUNDRED DOLLARS! STOP A RUN-AWAY NEGRO! TWO BROTHERS, LARGE REWARD!

The more I read, the sicker I felt. One handbill had come loose from the wall, and I ripped at the corner. The thing tore in half and the sound pleased me. I burnt the half I held in my hand and smiled as it curled and charred. I scratched at other papers, but mostly they stuck to the bricks.

Durn and blast it! I set the candle down and yanked out my knife, slashing at the papers. The knife hissed and scraped. Hacking the blade back and forth, up and down, I cut wide strokes all along that danged wall until nothing was left but bricks and shreds. Still I itched to finish the job.

The candle's flame guttered low. I lifted it and lit some of the loose bits of paper near the bottom, then stepped back, deep in the shadows, and watched as flames licked upward at the wall and charred every name.

I stood and watched until the last shred scorched and only wisps of smoke and ash remained. Good riddance. With my left hand I reached up and brushed along the bricks, then hollered with the pain of burnt fingers and yanked my hand away.

"Who's there? What's that? Do I smell smoke?" A man's voice called out. Footsteps sounded from inside the building.

Blessing my long legs, I lit out for the river without once looking back. When I got to the water, I knelt to ease my burns and wash, for surely I looked like a blacksmith covered with soot. But sore and dirty or not, I hadn't felt so full of rightness in a long time. I'd said my piece to Cincinnati.

Next morning I rose at first light and hitched up. Friend Coleman had described a back road that went straight to Winchester, Kentucky, and saved at least a day. The road was hilly and not much traveled, nor settled, but a day could make a difference to James, so I headed toward the river ferry the Quaker had suggested and guided my heavy wagon aboard.

No sooner had I stepped out on the Kentucky side of the river than the night's clouds opened up and it started to rain—a real deluge. The clouds poured out every drop of water they could find to welcome me to the state of Kentucky.

"Heavy rain, like this, it won't keep up, will it?" I asked the ferryman.

He shrugged. "Sometimes it will, sometimes it won't. Most summers the river don't hold enough water to float my boat. But then a year comes when we get storms from the south and water rises faster than a day's bread." He pulled an oilskin closer to his chest. "You got a sound piece of canvas on that wagon?"

"I do. Brand new and stretched tight."

"If you don't go touching no low spots on that cloth, you might just be all right. Unless it rains more than a day or so. Then nothin' going to keep the wet out. Come up a big rain like we had here last July, you might learn to swim."

"Thanks," I said. "Already know how. Hope I don't need it." But two days later, when it had rained solid without a pause and the road resembled mud soup, I began to wonder whether the Noah who had sent me on this trip might not be related to the real Noah in the Bible. And maybe I'd be better off with an ark.

My goods didn't get too wet, for I'd covered them with oilcloth, but I was soaked through. I'd planned to sleep under the wagon, but soggy grass and oozing mud made a poor mattress, so I had to shift crates and barrels to carve out a small niche for sleeping. After two days of slopping through mud and two nights of curling up tight in wet clothes, I felt like a muddy old hound dog and probably looked worse. The poor horses' coats were tangled and filthy.

"I just can't take it anymore, boys," I announced to them. "I've been looking for a barn all afternoon, but haven't seen a one. We'll have to stop here."

I pulled into a stand of pines, where thick branches shielded us from rain and old needles kept Charlie's and Sam's feet from the mud. Shucking off my clothes, I stood in the rain, even pulled out a bar of soap Mama had packed and washed myself all over, letting the warm rain rinse me from head to toe.

My boots and my traveling clothes were drenched, so I wrung out the worst of the water and tucked them under the wagon seat until I could find a town with a laundry or a day with sunshine.

Bare as a bird, I gathered armloads of grass for Charlie

and Sam to munch on and tried to brush them and untangle the knots from their manes and tails. By the time
I finished I'd gotten myself dirty again and had to take
another rain bath.

"What would Mama say if she saw me now?" I asked
Sam.

He munched grass as I scrubbed spots of mud from my
arms and legs. The minute the words were out, I knew
the answer. She'd call me a wild barbarian. That what
she'd called Tom and me when we were just little squirts
and we'd rampage through her garden or escape into the
backwoods with hoots and hollers.

Durn it, I missed the family then, missed the warmth
of our hearth on a cold, rainy day. I climbed up into the
wagon bed, dried myself as best I could on a piece of sack-
ing, and got out some soggy biscuits. Hard as it was to
admit, I even missed the runty little town of Atwater.
There, at least, I knew a few places a person could find
shelter from the storm.

It poured for another two days, making travel slow and
my thoughts as gray as the sky. Even when the rain
stopped the sun still didn't show his face. But it was
plenty warm—swampy-feeling, too. And I itched like the
dickens.

Somehow, I'd found poison ivy while traipsing around
naked and had developed itchy blisters on most of my
skin that I could reach and some places I couldn't. My
damp shirt and trousers only chafed at the rash.

If I was bad, my poor team fared worse. Charlie had

lost all his shoes to the muck, and Sam hobbled around like he'd gotten a bruise. A dry barn and a rest would help their feet, but I wasn't so sure about their coats. The hair on their rumps stuck up, and when I brushed it down, big old flakes of skin came off. I saw scabs under their coats, a sure sign of rain rot. That needed iodine, and I didn't have any.

What a pathetic excuse for a traveling man. I hadn't thought ahead about carrying medicine to tend my horses. I hoped the pair would make it to the nearest settlement and I'd somehow get to the farm where James lived, but deep in my belly, I worried that I might lose my animals and have to turn back in disgrace.

"Sorry, boys. I've been a danged fool. Put you through all this and made you pull a heavy load besides." I walked next to them and tried to encourage them. They slogged on with no complaints, but I saw misery in their eyes, and exhaustion.

All I could feel was tired and itchy. I was ready to quit myself and probably would have if I'd had a place to quit to. But as I stared ahead, all I could see was a muddy road, and the road behind was no better. Besides, I couldn't go home now; too much was at stake. So I slogged on.

Chapter 10

"What can I do for you, young feller? Ain't you got the sense to come in out of the rain?" The stable-man grinned at me through the dim twilight, showing crooked teeth. He had a full, bushy brown beard.

"Where am I?"

"This farm's within spitting distance of Winchester. You lost?"

"No. Just took longer on the road than I'd thought with all the rain. It's my team." I smacked at a patch of blisters on my side. "They kicked their shoes. Rain rot's got into their skin, too."

"Looks like you got a touch of rain rot yourself, boy.

You're all swelled up and splotchy. What'd you do, mess with a bush full of chiggers?" He led my team into the warm, dry stable and began to unhitch the waterlogged harness. I followed behind.

"Poison ivy." I fought the urge to scratch. If I dared start, I wouldn't be able to quit and I'd wear out my skin. Already a patch on my left arm had turned red and oozing, and all the boils had burst open.

I tried to shake off my itches. "The horses, sir. They need a blacksmith and medicine." I edged closer, ready to unbuckle Sam.

The man nudged me aside. "They mostly need a good drying out," he said. "You won't lose them or nothing." His voice got soft and kindly. "There's a smith comes by now and again. I'll send word for him. Like as not, he'll bring along some iodine for that rain rot, since he doctors horses when he shoes them. You need a place to stay! Near your goods?"

I nodded.

"You don't mind the smell of horses, do you, boy? Wife and me, we fixed up a room above the stables here. It ain't fancy, but you'll sleep dry and eat hearty, same as your team."

Eat the same as my team—oats and hay? If I said such a thing, he was sure to think my mind was cracked clean in two. He led me up a rough wood stairway and I followed, dumb as a sheep.

The room was plain, all right, with a few pegs for

clothes and a straw pallet on the floor. I felt like I was visiting the Queen of England, though, with four walls around me and no mud in sight.

"You haul what you need up from that wagon," he said. "I'll finish the horses and bring you some hot water and whatever I can scare up from the kitchen so late."

I really intended to do what he said, but something inside me just crumpled up when I saw that straw bed. I tumbled into it and reached for sleep before his feet sounded on the second step.

When I woke the next day, the sun had started downward in the sky. I itched all over and my belly growled like a hound dog at a stranger. It took a minute to remember where I was. Breathing in the safe smell of dry straw and horses, I realized I'd made it through six days of rain and muck and come close to Winchester. If I didn't see another rain cloud for a month, I'd be happy.

I threw cold water on my face from the bucket by the window and tried to make myself presentable. Clean clothes were below in my wagon, but I was too hungry to change.

I hurried down the steps and, for once, didn't stop to greet Charlie and Sam, just glanced their way to make sure they were still standing, and hurried out to the house. I knocked at the back door.

"Aren't you a sight, boy?" A large, freckled woman stood at the door, her hands on her hips. "Luke said to feed you till you groaned. Looks like a tall order. Come on in. Make yourself to home."

"I'll just sit on the back steps, ma'am. I'm real dirty."

"In case you haven't noticed, we run a stable here, not a Sabbath school. My kitchen has seen more mucky boots than clean. Now get yourself in here and eat. And what am I supposed to call you, young man? I can't keep saying 'boy.'"

"Will. William Spencer. Thank you."

"I'm Patricia Harlow. Patsy for short. Hope you like stew."

Her stew wasn't as tasty as Mama's, but I was in no mood to complain. I cleaned my plate three times, mopping up the gravy with big slabs of corn bread before I put down my spoon.

"Thank you, Mrs. Harlow. I really needed a good meal."

"That you did, William. Now for a bath. Water's heating in the kettle. Help yourself. Bucket's out back by the pump. You can use the washroom; just slosh down the floor after you're done. You have any dry clothes left?" She bossed me, just like Mama and Lucy. It made me feel right at home.

"Yes, ma'am. I'll check the wagon. And thank you again. I've been on the road awhile and a little kindness sure feels good."

"Tell you what'll feel good, you go out back behind the potato patch and you'll find some jewelweed. Orange flowers, about as big as a June bug. After you clean up, mash some of those stems and smear the juice on that ivy rash. It'll stop the itching for you."

63

"Thanks." I hoisted the kettle down from the stove and found my way to the washroom. With buckets of hot and cold water, a hunk of soap, and even a clean piece of toweling, that little stone-floored room felt like the bathing room of a fine hotel. I cleaned up, smeared jewelweed juice everywhere I could reach, and began to feel human again for the first time in a week.

When I headed back to the stable to check on my horses, their spirits had improved like mine. I threw my arm around Sam's neck and glanced at the tack hanging from a nearby nail. "Oh, Sammy, look at your harness. That rain was a killer." I tugged on the leather. Still sound, but I'd need a barrel of oil to keep it that way.

"Charlie, how are your feet?" I examined each hoof and found only one tear—a good trim and a new shoe would fix that.

"Checking your horses, are you, boy? That's good. You can tell a lot about a person by the way he treats his stock. Old Zeke will come tomorrow to shoe your pair and treat their coats. They'll be good as new in a few days. From the looks of things, so will you."

He nodded to me and left again. I felt good enough by then to hope we'd be fit for traveling, and soon. For despite the rain and my troubles, I had to get myself back on the road. More than three weeks had passed since Noah had sent me down here to find his family, and time was a-wasting.

Chapter 11

Dear Lucy,

I've never been so confounded in my whole life. Something's happened that goes against everything I believe, and I'm still trying to figure it out.

This fella and his wife run a stable on the edge of Winchester town and they took me in, me and Charlie and Sam, after we got soaked through in a big storm. They were kindly people. It was about all I could do to get them to allow me to pay for my bed and keep.

He kept saying that the way you cared for your stock was the sign of a real man. She kept saying how if she had a son on the road, she'd want him brought in out of *the rain, not left to drown like a cat. I finally talked her into a trade, but all she'd take was some cloth that lay on top by the wagon seat and got wetted by the rain.*

Sorry, Luce. I get mixed up telling this, but my mind's in a state. Let's see, I'll have stayed with them four nights and three days all told. The first day went by with no trouble, for I slept it away. Slept so long my brain went soft, for I sure wasn't prepared for what came next.

I stopped scribbling and set down my pen. The next part, it was so ugly, I couldn't figure how to explain it all to my sister but not give myself away in case anybody opened this letter. Durn and blast! I shook my head, but try as I might, couldn't shake away the faces, or the words.

It had started at supper that second night, when a whole crowd of colored folks gathered behind the house and a woman among them began to serve their supper.

"Didn't I tell you, boy?" the man said to me. "Got to take good care of your stock. I feed 'em real well. Give 'em meat twice a week. Keeps them real healthy." He pointed.

My mouth must have dropped right open when I realized he was talking about people—slaves—and he called them stock!

He wanted to keep them healthy and that made sense, for healthy folks would work a farm better than sick ones. But from his voice, it seemed like he had another meaning. I looked again at the people. Mostly women and children, with only one man. I'd heard of that before, from Noah. *"You don't need but a man or two for making babies."*

This man . . . The one who'd been so nice to me . . . I'd bet half the goods in my wagon that he ran a farm just like the one I'd come down here to steal James away from. What if this was the very farm, and one of those young fellas out there was James?

I blinked real hard and then glanced back at the house. It was painted a real soft yellow color, not white like the house Noah had sent me to. I wouldn't have to steal any folks away from this farm, but maybe I should.

That word, *stock,* made my back crawl. I liked my horses—sometimes they were better company than folks—but I didn't get animals and people mixed up. My ideas tumbled around plenty, though, before I lifted my pen again and tried to find the right words to explain it all to Lucy.

Lucy, I can't untangle it. I made a big mistake. I thought they were nice people. One part of me still thinks that. They were nice. But they keep geese, wild ones. They raise the young birds for market. They feed them all right, but they clip their wings and don't let them fly. I can't abide that. It's wrong.

Durn it, Luce, people should just stand still and behave the way they're supposed to behave. I want the bad people to stay bad and the good ones to stay good and not mix it up on me. Is that too much to ask? I feel just like Mama's poor old chickens must have felt back in May when we had that eclipse and day turned into night for a while.

Sure hope you have some answers and that you'll forgive me for hurling all these questions your way. Did I tell you the first letters I got were opened in Cincinnati? Be careful in what you write back and how, but please write soon.

Your upside-down brother,
William

Writing to Lucy improved my mood, not that I had any answers yet, but at least I was looking. Sprawled on the straw pallet, I pondered about good people and bad ones. I wanted to call myself honest and wouldn't cheat folks by a penny when I traded, but I was planning to steal slaves in a place where the law said owning folks was legal.

I started a letter to Elise but didn't know what to say, wondering what she'd make of me if she knew who and what I really was. Wondering which side of this terrible question she sat on and if I even dared to find out. Nope, not in the mood I was in. I folded my paper up for another day.

Questions pounded at me as I packed up all my dried-out merchandise and gear for the morning, and they still harried me later as the night sky blossomed with stars, but answers never came.

I didn't get much by way of answers the next morning either. Old Zeke, the smith who had treated Charlie and Sam, came by again, and this time I tried to get a closer look at him. He wasn't a white fella but an old colored man. I didn't know if he was a slave or free. And his name, Old Zeke, bounced around in my head. It sounded enough like Ezekiel that I wondered if he might be the man Noah had mentioned—someone I could count on for help. I figured I'd traveled far enough into Kentucky that he might be the right man. But I'd not been able to catch him alone to find out.

He checked both horses' feet first thing and declared them healthy. Then he got out his iodine bottle. "You best put some of this iodine on your arm, young mister."

He scrubbed the medicine onto Sam's broad rump. Sam stamped and jumped and tossed his head, so I knew that iodine stung plenty. And it was ugly. The previous treatments had turned both horses' coats a rusty shade of red. When the man turned to dose Charlie, I calmed Sam and buckled on his harness.

I shook my head. "Iodine's for horses. For the rain rot. This here's just poison ivy. I'm treating it with jewel-weed."

The old colored man looked me over carefully. "Jewel-weed be good enough for most your spots, but that patch on the arm look nasty. Whole arm might swell up and turn putrid without the iodine. You listen to Old Zeke, young mister. You think boils look pretty? Or cutting off an arm don't hurt?"

69

I wasn't afraid of a little sting, but losing an arm was another matter. "Smear it on." I swallowed hard and stuck out my arm, grateful that he poured the medicine on a clean rag instead of on the one he was using for the horses.

He dabbed at my arm.

My eyes burned. I bit back a yell. That iodine stung like the dickens, but I wasn't about to holler.

"Old Zeke . . ." I checked the barn to make sure we were alone. "Mr. Ezekiel?"

He set down the bottle and stared at me. "Where you get that name?"

I couldn't tell him straight out on the chance that he wasn't the right smith. "From somebody."

"What you want?" He practically growled the words out.

"I got a message. It's private. For some folks called James and Susannah. If you happen to know them."

He narrowed his eyes, then turned to the horses again and dabbed more iodine into Charlie's side.

"Please, Mr. Ezekiel. I need to find them fast."

"If I be your Mr. Ezekiel, and I ain't saying I am, how I gonna know you tell the truth?"

The arrowhead on its thong weighed heavy around my neck. "I might have a sign. But it's not just for anybody. Besides, how do I know you're Mr. Ezekiel?" I glared at him.

He just shrugged and dabbed Charlie.

The barn door creaked. Footsteps sounded behind me, so I shut my mouth, quick.

"Hey, Zeke." Mr. Harlow strode up to the stall. "You got them horses looking fine. This boy's talking about leaving this morning. You reckon his team will carry him?"

The smith nodded. "They'll do, if he don't push too far. If he heads my way, I can ride awhile with him, just to be sure."

I looked at him sideways but his brown face remained calm and gave me no sign. Durn and blast, I wasn't sure if I should trust Old Zeke or not. Before I'd found out the whole story about Mr. Harlow, the stableman, I might not have stopped to think, might have just jumped right in and followed my first inclination. But from what I could see, folks in these parts weren't always what they seemed. What was a stranger to do?

Chapter 12

Mr. Harlow spoke again. "We'd best settle up then, Zeke. You got a pass for me to sign?"

I wondered what that was about as I got out money to pay the blacksmith. "How much for the new horseshoes? I'd like to buy a spare bottle of iodine, too, to treat my animals if it rains again."

Old Zeke named a price, nodded, and got me a bottle. Mr. Harlow counted my money, then wrote the amount down on a slip of paper and signed it like he had the pass. That seemed peculiar.

"Thank you, mister," Old Zeke said. "You be ready to drive soon, young mister?"

Readier than he knew. "Wagon's all loaded; I just got to finish hitching up. I'd like your company, if you're willing."

"I'll see to my own horse, so I won't make you wait." He nodded again, then headed outside.

"Now, William, the wife's expecting you to come say goodbye. She packed a basket for you to carry along." Mr. Harlow reached out to shake my hand. "Don't be a stranger. Stop by again if you're on the roads near here."

"Yes, sir, thanks. You helped me a lot with the horses and all." I shook his hand and wondered, again, whether this man was my friend or my enemy. Neither name seemed to fit.

Of course, I wondered the same thing about Old Zeke when we'd traveled for nearly a mile and he hadn't talked about anything but horses. We ambled along, leading our animals along the country road real slow so as not to overtire my team.

Finally I couldn't stand it anymore and just blurted out my thoughts. "Are you really Mr. Ezekiel? Will you take me to Susannah and James?"

He shook his head at me, like maybe my poison ivy had spread to my brain. "Young mister, don't I hear you say you got a sign, but not for me? Well, maybe I got plans and notions, but not for you."

I snorted, but he'd given me a fair reply. If I wanted to hear anything more than shoes and harness, withers and hocks, I'd have to prove myself.

"All right. You want a sign, here it is." I watched his face as I reached inside my shirt and pulled out Noah's arrowhead.

He stared for a minute, then wiped sweat from his forehead. "Where you get that?"

"A fella. Used to live down here. You seen this before?"

"Maybe. This fella . . . he got a name? Where he be now?"

I kept my eyes fixed on his face. "Yeah, maybe he's got a name. Maybe he calls himself . . . Noah."

The man gave me the slightest of nods. And then he frowned. "He all right? This Noah fella?"

"He's fine. Hauled him a distance myself. He's heading for Canada, probably there by now."

He studied my face for the longest time, and my supply of patience was near used up. Then I remembered that song Noah had taught me. I pursed my lips and began to whistle.

He turned to me. "Where you get that tune?"

"Noah. I'd sing it for you, but the racket might bust your ears."

"Go ahead, sing awhile. I got strong ears."

I cleared my throat and took a breath.

"Ezekiel saw a wheel, spinning, right up in the middle of the air. A wheel in a wheel, spinning, up in the middle of the air." I shut my mouth and glared at him. "You hear enough?"

"Glory be," Old Zeke said. He sighed and looked at me kindly. "One more soul made free. I be your Ezekiel, young mister. Tell me about Noah."

Once my tongue got loose, I told about Noah hiding in the church loft, how I'd sent him on to Windsor, Ontario, and how he'd asked me to come south as a slave stealer. I explained about my sister Lucy, up in Canada for the summer, why she was there instead of home. Seemed like I couldn't stop talking after I finished that story, so my mouth rattled on about Atwater and the family, and the rainstorm and Cincinnati, and who knows what else.

My talking chewed up a whole bunch of miles, though, and I must have needed to spit out all those words, for once I'd said them, my heart felt lighter somehow.

"You cover a lot of miles for a young mister," he said when I'd finally run down. "You might like to know I'll take you direct to Susa. She got enough on her mind right now, without you show up and surprise her."

"Is it far?"

"Up the hills some. Rate we travel, we get there tomorrow in the afternoon. You hungry yet? I carry beans in my wagon."

"Sure, I could eat," I said. "But why don't we start on the food Mrs. Harlow packed? We can fix the beans when we stop for the night."

We found some shade and shared ham, cold potatoes, and corn bread. It seemed that the man relaxed a little with me, and that put a smile on my face.

Funny thing about travel—I hadn't expected this part. Living all my life in one place, people knew me. I'd never had to start fresh and show myself for others to measure.

On this trip, I'd not done too bad so far, but it felt strange and more than a little lonely.

I felt stranger still the next afternoon when Mister Ezekiel pulled his horse to a stop and faced me. "Young mister, I got to spit out some words before we get where we going."

"We're almost there?"

"Yep. If you aim to be a real peddler, you best do it right. Anyplace that keep slaves, you stop first at the master's house. If you got the time, and if the master say you can, you stop by the cabins late afternoon, after the people done with work."

"Sure, I can do that. Is that how I'll meet Susannah and James?"

"I find Susa for you," he said. "Just remember, every time you sell, go to the white folk first, then the cabins. Else there be trouble."

"All right."

"Another thing. Watch that tongue of yours." He shook his head like he was the schoolmaster and I was the class dolt. "Folks here won't take much shine to you if you jaw on about carrying my people north. Truth is, they'll look for a tree and a rope."

"I know," I protested. "I've been working the Railroad since I was twelve. I can keep my mouth shut."

He nodded. "Watch what you call me. White folks call me Zeke or Old Zeke. None of that Mister Ezekiel. No white folks ever call us mister or missus. You do and you stick out like a fox in the henhouse. And no Ohio talk.

All folks got to know is, you a peddler who sells goods, not where you come from or where you going to."

"All right. I'd rather talk to my horses anyway."

"That be right smart of you, Mister Will." He grinned. "Anything else we got to say before we among folks again?"

Mister Will. He'd finally used my name. That felt durn good. I thought for a minute. "Yes, sir. What was all that about a pass when Mr. Harlow signed papers? If I'm going to spend time around here, I'd better know how to act."

He patted his pocket. "We get passes from the master for travel. Me, being a smith, I travel a lot, so I get lots of passes. I see things. Know people. You understand?"

I began to. The man was a slave, but his skill gave him more freedom than most. Probably not much happened on these Kentucky farms that Mister Ezekiel didn't know about, which was why Noah had sent me south with his name. Some things still didn't make sense, though.

"If you know your way around, how come you're still here? Up north you could make a good living as a black-smith and be free. Why don't you run?"

He chuckled and shook his head. "Old man like me, run? I'd most likely get caught. Besides, knowing what I know, it makes me useful to folks in trouble. If I travel north, who helps them find the way?"

That sure made sense. The smith did here what I did in Ohio—worked the Railroad—helped people north. "One more question, then I'll stop jawing, sir. What about the money? Why did Mr. Harlow write that down?"

"I do the work for you on his farm. He write it so my master get his share, fair and true."

"Your master? He gets some of your blacksmith money?"

"Half for him, half for me. I may not travel north, but I can save to buy out my freedom and my wife's, too."

"But that's not right." I frowned. "Your master didn't work for the money. You did. You should get all of it."

He shook his head again. "They be *what should* and they be *what is*. I live with *what is*. Like I say, you best put a lock on that tongue. Else you get in trouble so bad even my iodine won't fix."

With that warning fresh in my mind, I followed Mister Ezekiel as he turned his wagon up a narrow dusty lane toward a trim white house and a girl called Susannah.

I couldn't help wondering about James, though. It didn't make sense that Mister Ezekiel kept talking about Susannah but hadn't mentioned James's name even once.

Chapter 13

As Mister Ezekiel suggested, I headed for the white house and the white folks, trusting him to hunt out Susannah and find a way for us to meet up. Meanwhile, since this would be my first try for a sale, I had to figure out how to look like a real peddler and not just a green boy. I yanked my hat farther down on my head, glad that I'd gotten it so wet—it didn't look so new or raw. I wasn't sure about the rest of me, but at least I was big enough to be taken for a man.

I reined the horses to a stop and climbed down to tie them to a split-rail fence. Taking a deep breath, I headed toward the back door. Before I got there, an old colored woman pushed out and hurried away. She had her hands over her face, and I thought I heard her moan but couldn't be sure.

Mister Ezekiel had warned me and his words echoed in my ears. The old woman wasn't my business. Still, I waited a few more minutes before I knocked on the back door, to let things calm down inside that house, or maybe inside myself.

When I did knock, the response came quick. A woman with pasty white skin and pale hair opened the door. "Yes?"

I tugged off my hat. "I'm Will Spencer, ma'am. Selling goods from my wagon—cloth and house goods, salt and spices. Would you need anything today?" I grinned at her like a fool. My palms felt greasy with sweat and a few spots of poison ivy on my side still itched.

"Got house goods, have you? You a peddler, then?"

"Yes, ma'am. I've got a fine supply. Pots and pans. Cloth and ribbons and buttons, too, if you've a mind to look them over. Hot as it is now, fall's coming and some ladies like to get a start on their sewing."

I said this as if I knew about sewing. In fact, I was rattling on worse than a busted wagon wheel, but Papa had told me to put on the charm to make a good sale and I was doing my best.

"I will have a look," she said. "High summer we're so busy with the fields and the gardens, there's no time for a trip to Winchester. And just this morning my largest mixing bowl got broken. I'd say you've come at the right time, boy."

She stuck her head into the kitchen and called to somebody inside, then followed me to my wagon.

Since she'd already admitted needing a bowl, I showed her them first. Then cloth and buttons and everything she might want. She picked out a little of this and a little of that, asking prices every time.

"You carry any heavy dark cloth? Something that won't wear through, nor show the dirt?"

She was going to make some good solid purchases after all. Not bad for my first try at selling. I grinned. "Yes, ma'am. I've got dark blue and brown and gray and black. I could cut you some of each."

She shook her head. "I'll need a whole roll, color don't matter. Just make sure it's sturdy and not too dear."

I hauled out some heavy stuff in dark blue and brown, for those were the rolls closest to the top.

"Which one's cheaper?" she asked.

I looked around. The farm seemed prosperous enough. She wore a nice dress with no mends showing, so I figured she was just careful with her money, not poor. If this farm wife wanted a bargain, she'd get a bargain.

"Think I could do a little better with the brown," I said. "The supplier gave it to me for a good price. And since you don't want me to cut it . . ." There. I'd made it sound tempting, but hadn't actually told a lie, for the supplier *had* given me a good price on the brown. She didn't have to know he'd given me the same price on the rest. This peddling was tricky business.

"I told you already color don't matter. It's just for

81

them." She tilted her head off in the direction the old woman had headed. "Now could I look at that fancy light blue wool once more?"

Just for them? For the slaves.

I bit my lip, tempted to yank all my goods back into my wagon and whip up the team without selling a single pin. But I couldn't. First off, if I hauled myself out of there without finishing the sale, it would make the woman suspicious. More important, Susannah was nearby.

I added up the total on a scrap of paper. The woman was counting out money to pay me when a pale little girl came up and tugged on her skirt. "Mama? Kin I get a ribbon?" She grinned up at me and stood on tiptoe to look inside my wagon.

"Hush, Mary. I'm spending too much already."

"But, Mama . . ."

I reached into the box with the ribbons. "Mary, what color do you like? I've got a sister Miranda who's just a little bigger than you. I sent her a blue one. Would you like a blue?"

Her mother started to shake her head.

"I won't charge you for it, ma'am. You've bought plenty. I'd like her to have the ribbon." That was the honest truth. The little girl did remind me of my sister, and I liked making a present for her, even if her folks were slave owners. Wasn't right to blame a child for the sins of the parents, so I passed her a nice length of blue ribbon.

"I thank you for coming by and for your kindness to

Mary. Will you stay for a meal? Our people will finish work soon, and some of them may have a few pennies saved up. You could visit the cabins after supper. What did you say your name was?"

"Will, ma'am. Will Spencer, peddler." I followed her toward the house, carrying all her purchases, and wondered if she'd have invited me to sit at her family's table if she knew who I really was—Will Spencer, thief.

Chapter 14

I spent an uncomfortable hour at the supper table with the family—Mr. John Merrick, his wife, Amelia, and their children. Uncomfortable because I had to watch every word that came out of my mouth so that I didn't give anything away. Lucky for me Mama had taught me not to talk with a full mouth. I kept shoveling in pork and potatoes, so I didn't have to contribute much to the conversation, just asked Mr. Merrick if I could show my goods to his slaves.

With his approval, after supper I made my way back to the row of log cabins that stood south of the barn. Mister Ezekiel had told the people I'd be coming, so they were ready. In fact, instead of me visiting one cabin at a time, a flock of women and children came to the wagon, curious as birds.

I peered around, trying to figure which one might be Susannah, but hadn't a clue. Nor did they give me time to think or wonder. They pressed close to the wagon.

Some had coins, others carried jars of preserved fruit, or dried meat, or skins for trading. That was fine, for I I'd planned to trade some just to feed myself, and I'd met a merchant back in Cincinnati who would buy the skins.

"How much, how many, what color? Ain't you got a better price?" I hadn't expected so much business, but to be honest, I enjoyed it. Lengths of cloth and trimmings sold well, and so did tobacco for the couple of men who wandered by when the worst of the crowd eased.

"Miss Delight, she ask if you stop by her cabin before you leave," one of the men said. "She don't feel too good just now."

"Sure. Which one?" I hoped this was my chance to see Susannah.

"Last one, up by the fence." He pointed and I nodded in thanks.

When I got to the door, an old woman waited, the same old woman who'd hurried from the main house earlier. She was small and thin, with soft white hair pulled back into a knot at her neck. Her face was dark brown and wrinkled, and she looked at me without a smile.

"Miss Delight?"

"You the peddler boy?"

"Yes."

"You got any calico? Might could use a piece."

"I'll bring some into your cabin."

I carried five rolls through the door, which she closed behind me. Setting the cloth on a rough wood table, I unfolded each to let her see the colors while my eyes wandered around the room. I'd never seen a slave cabin before nor set foot in one until that very minute.

In fact, it looked an awful lot like some of the older houses in Atwater. Made of split logs, it had a dirt floor and windows with wood shutters, but no glass. Besides the table, she had a straw mattress off to one side, a bench, a shelf with some cooking gear and dishes, and a hearth with a three-legged pot for cooking. It wasn't a big house, but I did see a rough ladder, which probably led to a loft like the one I slept in at home with Tom.

"Peddler boy, you have something else to show me?"

"You don't like these colors?"

"I ain't talking about calico. I be looking to *see* something."

"Oh. Sure." I reached into my shirt and drew out the rawhide thong, slipped it off my neck, and handed it to her. "I'm hoping to see *somebody* myself."

She studied the arrowhead. "Susa," she called softly. "Come down now, gal."

A girl climbed slowly down the ladder, like she wasn't sure if she wanted to or not. Puzzling, for I'd expected a bit of excitement from her if she was truly Noah's sister.

The girl edged closer.

"Sit," the old woman ordered. She lowered herself to the bench.

The girl settled onto the floor, cross-legged, and I did the same.

"He come, like Ezekiel say. Now we listen. Go on, peddler boy. Tell what you know." She passed the necklace to the girl, who clutched it in her hand, examined it for a moment, and then sniffed. Miss Delight took it back and stuck it in her pocket.

My neck felt naked somehow without the leather thong. I rubbed it, trying to study the girl's face without her noticing. Tracks of wetness ran down her reddish brown cheeks. "Susannah? My name is Will Spencer. I brought you news of your brother."

She stared at me before she spoke, with dark eyes that held back more than they showed. "Which one?"

"Noah, of course. He's safe by now, escaped and up in Canada. He sent me down here to find you and James and bring you up to join him."

New tears appeared on her cheeks, and she didn't even try to brush them away, just let them run on down and drip onto her dress.

"Please, Susannah. Don't cry. I'm sure Noah's safe. I'll steal you out of here and take you to him. Get James to come down and we'll make plans."

She shook her head at me and sighed.

"Miss Delight, please. Tell her. She should be happy, not sad."

"Hush, boy. You don't know what we know—"

"What is it?" I interrupted. "What's wrong?"

"James." Susannah spoke the name like it burned her throat.

"You come too late, peddler boy," Miss Delight explained. "James run off five, maybe six nights back. We don't know if he safe or in trouble. We don't know if he alive or dead."

At those words Susannah jumped up, ran for the ladder, and disappeared from sight into the loft. I could hear her crying.

"No!" I slumped and covered my face with my hands. "Why did he run, Miss Delight? What are we supposed to do now?"

The old woman began her tale in a deep, sad voice. It sounded a lot like the story Noah had told me weeks ago. Just before the rains came, news had traveled from one farm to the next. A soul driver was on the road, buying up boys as young as ten or eleven. Paid good prices, too, if they were dark like James, not mixed-blooded or troublesome. So James and two others had run, in the middle of that downpour. Headed north. No word yet.

During the telling, Susannah climbed back down her ladder. Now she sat near the hearth and stared out a window into the darkening evening, not quite with us, but not hiding anymore, either.

"Do you usually hear? Do you get word if somebody's run away?" I asked.

"Maybe yes, maybe no." The old woman looked stern.

"Most times if we hear, it be bad news. Somebody get catched, get brought back and punished. Whip with the cowskin. Lose a finger, lose a toe. Get sold, quick, before he run again."

"So if you haven't heard, it means he hasn't been caught?" I tried to make my words hopeful, but my memory got in the way. I could see that terrible wall back in Cincinnati and those greedy men who read the notices and got their dogs ready to hunt. To hunt for James and his two friends.

"We don't hear, it just mean we don't hear," the woman said. "It mean we got to wait. And pray."

"No!" I stood and paced, unable to sit still and hear any more. "Waiting and praying, that won't do any good. James is headed north. If he's lucky, he'll get there and get free. I've got to get Susannah free too."

I turned to the girl. "Please. Come north with me. Tonight. I'll hide you in my wagon. Come north and I'll take you to Noah. I promised. I can't let him down. You've got to come."

"Don't you tell me what I got to do, peddler boy," she said.

"But, Susannah—"

"Can't leave if James gets caught and needs me here," she said. "I got to wait and pray."

"But—"

"You have family?" she demanded. "Brothers and sisters?"

"Sure." That was a big part of the reason I was here, for

I had brothers and sisters of my own and could imagine how Noah must be worrying.

"You gonna leave if one of them need you? You just run off and take care of your own sweet self, even if your brother in danger?"

I thought back to when Lucy had gotten into deep trouble. I'd stuck to her like a cocklebur, unwilling to let her travel alone even when I knew it was for the best. She'd had to pry me off. I'd do the same for Tom or Miranda.

"That's different," I said, feeling my face get hot. "In my family we can go where we want. It's not dangerous for us. We're not slaves."

"Danger or not, family matters. Maybe more for us than for you. I lost plenty of kinfolk in my life. I ain't letting go of what little family I got left, and you can't make me."

"Please, Susannah, at least you've got to think about it."

"Nothing to think on. I got to be here if James come back. I got to tend him if they whip him and bind up whatever they chop off him for running. That what I got to do." She turned her face to the wall.

Miss Delight raised a finger to her lips and tilted her head toward the door.

I wasn't wanted here. Tarnation! I kicked at the dirt floor and crossed the room, shoved open the door, and headed for my wagon. Dang that Noah anyway. How many walls did a fella have to bang his head against before he said quit?

Chapter 15

I was tempted to leave right then and never come back. I climbed into my wagon and drove until I was outside the fences that marked the Merricks' farm. I made camp there for the night, under a wide beech tree where bats flapped in and out of the shadows as the stars came out.

If I'd had some light, I'd have written to Lucy for comfort, to Mama and Papa for steadying, or to Elise for hope. But in the darkness I couldn't write to anybody, so I spent a long night there alone, unsteady in my mind and about as hopeless as a fella could be.

By the time morning dawned, I decided to make one last try with Susannah, so I headed back toward that row of log cabins. People were up, hauling water, when I got to the front of Miss Delight's cabin. "Susannah? You here? I got to talk to you again."

She came to the door, and I was surprised to see she was tall, near as tall as me. Last night we hadn't been standing up at the same time. I lowered my voice to a whisper. "Susannah, please. Won't you come with me? I need you to."

She looked at me with sad brown eyes and slowly shook her head from side to side.

"Please, Susannah . . ."

"Well, what's this? Visiting awful early in the morning, ain't we?"

I spun around. John Merrick, the owner of the farm, stood two paces behind me wearing an ugly grin. He was a tall, skinny man with red cheeks.

"I . . . Um . . ."

He wiped his hands on his overalls. "I know what you're doing, boy. And believe me, you're going about it all wrong. You being from up north and all, guess you don't know our ways."

"Your ways?"

He nodded and his grin got even wider and uglier. "Fact is, you've asked the wrong person, boy. You want to spend a little time with Susa, here, all you got to do is ask me. She ain't the one who gets to decide."

No! He couldn't mean what I thought he meant. Out of the corner of my eye, I could see people gathering from the cabins. They watched like we were putting on quite a show. I needed to escape.

He chuckled. "Good-looking boy like you. Well, if you want to plow that field, fine with me." He hooked his thumbs in his overall straps and stood with his elbows out, acting for all the world like a barnyard rooster.

I wanted to plug up my ears as John Merrick went on talking.

"Tell you what, you come back tonight. Can't let you bother her while she's working, but tonight will be just fine. Any night you want. Who knows, you might just help me grow my business."

"I . . . But . . ." I curled my fingers so tight the nails stung my palms.

"No need to go red in the face, son. You're full-grown." He stepped closer to the door. "Be nice to him, Susa. You're getting on past fifteen and you ain't catched yet. That don't change pretty soon, you might be taking a boat ride." He slapped his leg, laughed again, punched me in the shoulder, and strode off toward the main house.

I stood there, shaking from head to foot, and watched him go.

Somebody nudged at my back. Miss Delight. "Why you stand there, peddler boy? You hear the master. Get yourself back after we finish work." She glared at me, and I didn't dare disobey her or the man who owned this place and these people.

I turned back toward the doorway to mumble some sort of apology to Susannah, but she just stood there as stiff and unmoving as a hickory post. And the audience to our drama stood just as still, watching.

As much for them as for myself, I loosed my fists and stuck my hands into my pockets casual-like, as if things like this happened to me every week. Somehow, I found my voice. "Sure. Fine. Tonight, then. And I'll bring you something, Susannah. Something for supper."

I climbed up into my wagon, snapped the reins, and lit out for the main road like a pack of wolves were chasing me. After the ugly things I'd heard from John Merrick's mouth, I'd have preferred the company of wolves.

Driving calmed me. I stopped at several houses along the way and traded. In spite of the morning's dreadful start, my business went fine. I couldn't help enjoying the jingle of coins in my hand as women paid for their goods. I was turning into a real peddler. Cloth, needles and thread, buttons, those were sure sellers and I had plenty.

Elise had given me good advice about stocking for fall and winter. But as I brought her face to mind, my cheeks went hot with shame. I didn't know what it would take to wipe John Merrick's nasty accusations from my memory. What he'd said sure made me feel like a rotten person, even if it wasn't true.

I kept selling and pushed my horses pretty hard, so we were all drooping when we finally pulled up to Miss Delight's cabin that evening. People sat out on their steps, watching for me. Made my cheeks go all hot again.

After feeding and watering my team, I turned them loose in a fenced pasture back behind the cabins. People still looked when I went inside the house carrying a jar of blackberry jam I'd traded for that morning.

"Miss Delight. Susannah." I stepped in and closed the door. "I'm sorry about this morning. I didn't mean for any of that to happen."

"Hush, now," the old woman said. "It be for the best."

"For the best? No! You don't understand."

"Oh, I understands. If he think you come here to pester Susa, that mean you can keep coming here."

"But it's not right. People are watching. They'll think bad things about her." I turned. "Susannah, I'm sorry."

"It don't matter."

Something inside me exploded. I kicked out and my boot made contact with the bench, sending it across the room.

"It does matter!" I bit my tongue to keep from shouting. "I would never ask you to do something like that. We don't even know each other. You don't like me. How could we . . . ?"

"Set down, you young folk," Miss Delight said. "I be fixing beans and corn bread. Susa, you explain this young man what he need to know."

Susannah retrieved the bench and set it upright again. She sat down while I leaned against the cabin wall.

"You say Noah send you . . ." She wouldn't look me in the eye. "That make me think he tell you about us. About here."

"He told me some." I studied her fine, strong profile.

"About James, how he might get sold. He didn't say you were in trouble."

"I ain't in trouble. *He* just want me to start babies. I got to pretty soon, else I get sold too."

"So he can make you . . . you know . . . with anybody?"

She nodded. "He own me. What you think, peddler boy? I some fancy white girl who get a fine wedding first? He say lay with a man, I lay with him. I get used to it."

I wanted to get out. Out of the cabin and the farm and the whole durned state of Kentucky. But as much as Susannah's words made me want to run, they also gripped me tight right where I stood. I had to stay here until she got word from James or until she gave up on him. One way or another, I had to get her free. Not for Noah's sake anymore either, but for hers. And for my own self-respect.

Chapter 16

"What we going to do is this," Miss Delight said as she ladled out beans and passed corn bread. "Peddler boy, he do his work. Ride around the hills, sell to the folks. Little trip here, little trip there. We wait for James."

She turned to me. "You come back here every week. Go north a ways, come back. Go east, come back. Master, he think you come visit Susa, he don't care. If we gets word, we packs for travel. If James come back here, caught, we figure that out when the time come. Susa?"

She nodded.

"You got a tongue, gal?"

"Yes, ma'am. I do what you say. If we hear James makes

free, I go too. If he come back, I heal him up, whatever his troubles."

They'd left out one part—if James didn't come back and didn't send word. If I brought that up, I knew Susannah would go all stiff and wooden again, so I decided to wait and hope for the best. As long as I played along with old John Merrick's nasty mind, I wasn't putting myself or them in any immediate danger. Besides, I didn't have to leave the area until I'd emptied my wagon of goods, and that could take weeks.

Later that night, I lay wide awake on a straw pallet beside Miss Delight's hearth. The old woman snored lightly, but sleep wouldn't come my way. I got to my feet, slipped out the front door, sat on the step, and stared at the summer sky. Maybe I should just leave soon and return to my wagon to sleep, instead of staying here all night.

In the distance a dog barked. Down the row of cabins a baby cried and then stopped. Three stars, or four, showed beyond the trees. It might be late enough to leave.

Behind me, the door creaked and I turned. "Susannah?"

"Can't sleep."

"Me neither. What that man said, Susannah. It's all wrong. I'm not like that. I've got sisters and I'd pound on anybody who treated them like—"

"Shhh. Ain't your fault."

I lowered my voice to a whisper. "It is if I can't get you out of here."

"Can't we talk about something else? Please?"

"Sure." But I couldn't think of anything to say that didn't include either John Merrick's ugly words or running away.

"How you like peddling?"

"Real fine so far. Hey . . . do you know much about the area? The nearby farms? Wouldn't hurt to know where to sell my goods. And I need to get into Winchester to the post office."

"I know some places," she said. "They take me into the town sometimes. What you want to know?"

It was the first real conversation I'd had with her, and as we talked I mapped out a week's worth of travel.

"Thanks," I said. "Hope I don't get lost."

"I thank you," she said, her voice so soft I almost didn't catch the words. "You come here from Noah. How he be keeping?"

"He seemed real fine to me. I left him off in Ravenna, Ohio, with a Quaker doctor. By now he's safe in Canada, farming, most likely."

"I hear they don't make slaves in Canada. He the hired boy?"

"I don't think so. Anyway, he wouldn't be staying with white folks. He's probably with a family who escaped just like he did."

"Folk like me own a farm?" Her voice grew louder and she stared me square in the face, testing for truth.

I nodded and looked up—stars filled the sky and I pointed to one. "That's why I want to carry you north,

99

following that very star. If you and James can get up to Canada with Noah, you can get a farm too. Some of the land's free, the rest you pay for over ten years. You can stay with a settler family at first. They'll help you."

"Free slaves. Free farms. You make this up?"

"No. It's the exact truth. Some people call Canada the promised land. From what I've seen, they're not far wrong."

She didn't say much. But me, once I'd started talking, I just kept going. Told her about our life in Atwater. The Railroad. Lucy. Pretty soon she was peppering me with questions. Told me some about her life and her brothers. We must have talked all night, for we were still rattling on when the sun pinked the edges of the sky.

"Sorry, Susannah, I kept you awake. You're going to have a hard day, all tired out."

She shook her head, and I could see the start of a grin in the dim morning light. "People gonna laugh. They joke me about you before, now they say you keep me up all night."

"Oh, no! I didn't even think—"

"No. If they say those things, we get time to plan. I get to hear more about that promised land. Peddler boy, next time, you bring me something fancy. We make those people think you got a strong feeling for me."

"How about ribbons for your hair? My sisters like them."

"You got pretty colors? I like pretty colors, peddler boy."

100

"I'll bring you one of every color I've got," I promised.

"And you don't want nothing back in trade?"

I shook my head. "Not like *he* said. But . . . well . . . I've got a name, Susannah. You could stop calling me peddler boy. I'm William Spencer. My friends and family mostly call me Will."

She shrugged. "I never call a white person by name before, but I can try."

I grinned at her and stuck out my hand. "Fair trade, Susannah?"

She looked undecided for a minute, then stuck her hand out and shook mine firmly. "Fair trade," she agreed. "William."

Chapter 17

I traveled and traded for more than a week, ending up in the town of Winchester, Kentucky, where three letters waited for me at the post office. Outside of town in a shady grove of locust trees I leaned against a rough trunk and opened the letters.

One was from Mama and Papa, full of farm news and thanks for the packet. Two came from Lucy. Her first one told news of her teaching and the folks she was staying with. The second she'd written in a kind of code, even though this time my letters hadn't been unstuck.

Dear Tangled-up Brother Will,

Just received your letter. Are you turning literary on me? I'd be delighted. Actually, this letter will probably be more like philosophy, for I've enjoyed my studies of that subject at the college.

You ask big questions, Will. Good and evil. I'm as confused as you. If it's any help, people have worried over these ideas for hundreds, even thousands of years. They've written books and books on the subject.

Here's how I try to think of it. I'm teaching people to read and work numbers this summer, and there are two little girls in my class. One is stronger and more outspoken. She reads well and has a quick memory for the poems and recitations I give her. The other child stumbles and mixes up the words. But with numbers she's as sharp as a crow's eye.

What I'm trying to say, Will, is that some people are good at some things and not at others, at least in school. But I suspect school and life aren't so different. A man could be generous with his family and friends but unfriendly, even cruel, with others. He could be kind to horses but uncertain and awkward with his fellows. Why? I don't know. Does any of this make sense?

I hope I haven't further perplexed you, dear brother. As a child, you would plunge directly into the pond, so you were either soaking or bone dry. You preferred absolutes, so words like partial and halfway may not sit *comfortably on your shoulders. But the world isn't always as we might like, and people come in an amazing variety of temperaments.*

There. I have done it. I'm sure I have now tied at least ten more knots in the tangle you are wrestling with. Perhaps you should have written instead to Miranda, who is sure to be more certain of everything at the ripe age of nine than I at nineteen. But do write again about this, or other thoughts you might have, for I enjoy such discussion with my no longer childish brother.

Shall I send on your questions to my good friend Jeremiah? Yes, we continue to correspond. He is spending the summer in Ohio and plans to visit me in Canada before he returns to the college at Swarthmore. We will travel back across the lake together in August, with his sister, Charity, acting as chaperone. Isn't that amazingly proper for a sinner such as myself? Truly, I can't wait, for letters are a poor substitute for the company of dear friends and absent brothers.

Fondly,

Lucy

I read Lucy's letter twice, then folded it up and sighed. I'd hoped she'd make life plain to me—who was good and who was bad—to send me a road map, clear and easy to read. What she'd sent was more like a geography book, full of complications.

I pulled up a blade of grass and chewed on the sweet

white part at the end, still not sure what to think. Blue jays called down at me, mocking my confusion. I picked up a pebble and tossed it at the jays, but they only flew to a higher branch and continued to scold.

That last part of the letter made me smile, though. Good old Jeremiah Strong. I'd about given up on him once he and Luce went their separate ways to college. Now he was headed up to Canada for a visit and would cart my sister and her belongings back to Oberlin.

Best part of all, they needed Charity Strong for a chaperone. A cold hearth sure didn't need a firescreen. I slapped my thigh. With a little luck, there might be a wedding next May, once Lucy and Jeremiah finished their studies. Maybe I should help the romance along. I'd give a lot to see my sister settled and happy instead of on her own so much, even if it meant I'd have to put on my durned Sunday suit for her wedding.

I'd have to get real good at writing Lucy letters, even write direct to Jeremiah's sister, Charity. Tell her to do a pitiful poor job as chaperone. Fire up those embers some. Bet she'd like to see a wedding at least as much as I would.

While my mood was still sweet, fine, and soft in the heart, I got out more paper and wrote to Elise.

July 10, 1854

Dear Elise,

You said I might write to you, so I am. After two weeks in Kentucky now I've found my way around. The hills are real green, with little streams and lots of forests. I'm sitting here under a locust tree right now, with the sound of a creek and waterfall not far off.

Outside Cincinnati a terrible rainstorm came up— you probably felt some of that water too, didn't you? I picked up a wicked case of poison ivy rash, but that's healing now. Well, once my horses and I dried out, and the itching stopped, I began trading and guess what? I'm good at it and I like talking to folks and seeing new places. They welcome me and I help some, for folks can't always get what they need if they live too far from town. Of course, part of the reason my goods sell real well is that I got some fine advice about what to stock. The cloth and ribbons you suggested are more than half gone. Thank you for your good suggestions.

Thanks, too, for agreeing to have supper with me when I return. Now that I've spent time on the road, I understand how important true friends really are, for the road can get mighty quiet.

Your wandering friend and peddler,
William Spencer

Chapter 18

Late Saturday afternoon, tired and dirty, I returned to the Merrick farm. After seeing to my horses and washing up in a little creek, I pulled out a fistful of ribbons in different colors for Susannah—to wear her down with presents and talk of Windsor while I emptied my wagon with trading.

As I stepped up to Miss Delight's cabin, loud voices wailed from inside. All I could imagine was that James had been caught and drug back here to be punished.

It took some courage to knock at that door. Susannah opened it and nodded for me to come in. I looked around. No James. Miss Delight sat on the bench, rocking and wailing. Another woman sat beside her and wrung out a cloth, then tried to place it on Miss Delight's cheek, but Miss Delight pushed it away and hollered even louder.

"After all these years! With her shoe! I never been treated like that."

"What happened?" I asked Susannah. We stood in the doorway, fixed in place.

"Not sure. Missy smacked Miss Delight with her shoe."

"Missy?" I asked.

"Master's wife. The Missus."

I stared. Miss Delight had to be way past sixty, old enough to be my grandmother. I walked over to the bench and sat at the feet of the two women. "Miss Delight. It's me, William. What happened?"

She sniffed at the sight of me, but the wailing stopped. At first I thought it was because she saw me as a friend, but she hardly knew me. More likely she didn't want to show her hurt in front of a white person. Couldn't much blame her for that. I spotted what looked like a dark welt on her right cheek.

"Go on now, Bess. I be fine. You got a supper to cook."

Her friend tried once more with the wet cloth, and this time Miss Delight took it and held it to her face.

"I bring you something, hear. You ain't cooking this day."

Miss Delight nodded and the woman called Bess left us alone.

"What happened?" I asked again. "How did you get hurt?"

Susannah sat next to Miss Delight and put an arm around her.

"That Missy. I fix the table for they supper—set out the plates, all the silverware. I drop a cup and it chip, not bad, just a little. Missy hear and come rushin' in. She pick up the cup, see the chip. 'My Mama's good china,' she say. She fling that cup against the wall and it break in a hundred pieces. I say sorry, but she don't care about sorry. She take off her shoe and smack me, this cheek and then this one, again and again. 'Get out my house,' she say, and I run. Oh, Lordie, it be a hard life, this Kentucky." She slumped as if the telling had worn her out.

Susannah hugged her tighter and crooned softly as if rocking a baby.

I jumped to my feet and paced. A cup! A durn chipped cup was all it took for an old woman to get beaten with a shoe! This Kentucky was more than hard, it was evil. I kicked at the stones of the hearth—it felt good—but I really wanted to kick Missy, to scatter her precious china and stomp it.

Susannah came up to me and pulled on my arm. "Please, William. You ain't helping by wearing a rut in our floor."

I took a deep breath and tried to settle my temper. "Sorry, Miss Delight, but that woman should be horse-whipped. What can I do?"

"Nothing."

"Nothing? Please, I want to help."

"Don't you understand? They owns me. They do what

109

they want. You can't do nothing for me. But you can take this gal up north. Get her away to a place where nobody going to smack her face with no shoe."

Susannah's chin came up with a stubborn look to it. "I'm waiting for James," she said.

"Noah didn't wait for you, did he? Or for James? You can wait your whole life and still your brother don't come. You got to make free. I hear from James, I send him on, or Ezekiel will."

"I can't."

"You got to. Look, gal, you got one brother safe and free. That more than some folk ever get. You count your blessings and get north soon as this boy ready to travel."

Miss Delight's words seemed to grab Susannah's attention, and I held my breath waiting to see if she might change her mind. But as I watched her face, I could see the uncertainty leave, replaced by a familiar stubborn frown. If having an old woman beaten on the face with a shoe wasn't enough to make Susannah leave, what was?

"Can't leave, Miss Delight. For James and for you. I got to stay and take care of you now. That Missy . . ." She scowled.

"You leave James and me to the good Lord," Miss Delight said firmly.

Then it hit me. I'd been so dense. My wagon was plenty big.

Striding to the window, I looked out—not a soul in sight. I lowered my voice to a bare whisper. "Miss

Delight, is it true Mister Ezekiel could get word to James if he comes back?"

"Ezekiel, couple other folks in the cabins. We got our ways."

"All right. Then here's what we'll do. Give me two or three weeks to sell my goods and empty my wagon. Then I'll come back here for you, Susannah, and you, too, Miss Delight. Get word to Mister Ezekiel for James to head up to Windsor, Ontario, Canada West. And get ready, for when I come back we'll leave in a hurry, probably in the middle of the night."

They looked at each other for a moment, as if deciding who would get the first turn to disagree with me. Then Miss Delight spoke. "Can you do it? Can you carry a old woman like me? How you keep them from finding me?"

"Wagon's got a false bottom, special-made."

"You can fit two?"

"I fit eight folks once. It won't be the most comfortable trip you ever took, but you can ride north. I've carried lots of folks before."

She crossed the room and stood looking out the window. "I spend my whole life in this place, owned. Guess I can take a little hard riding for freedom." She turned to Susannah. "What about you, gal? I'm going. With you or without you."

In the late-afternoon shadows, I saw worry on Susannah's face, and pain. "You really leave without me?"

Miss Delight looked like she'd been carved from stone.

"Noah left by hisself. So did James. If they can do it, I can do it. How about you, Susa? You got the gumption?"

We stood there for what seemed like a long time without speaking, without even moving. Finally Susannah sighed. "I . . . I guess I'll go." She touched her cheek lightly with her fingertips. "I won't stay around here all by myself and wait for somebody to smack my face with no shoe." She turned to me. "While you gone, I be wearing out my knees. I pray every night. How about you, William? You going to pray for my brother too?"

"I'll pray for all of us, Susannah. I promise."

And I meant it. I'd bend my knees every single night and ask God to get us out of here safely. With two runaways riding in my wagon and weeks of travel to reach Canada, we'd need all the help we could get.

Chapter 19

I must have done a fine job of praying or else the Lord had extra time on His hands. The goods from Cincinnati flowed out from the wagon and money and skins flowed back in at every stop.

I traded for quilts from the hill women, for they'd offer my passengers warmth and comfort on the trip north. I traded for corn whiskey, too, and shuddered to think what Mama'd say, but whatever it took to empty that wagon of merchandise, I'd do it. And when the tavern owner back in Cincinnati paid for the corn whiskey, I'd give the money to Miss Delight and Susannah to give them a start up in Canada. Even Mama might approve of that—turning the Devil's work to the Lord's blessing. The notion pleased me.

I ventured east and south, through clear days and rainy ones. As I pointed the wagon toward the Merrick farm, I stopped one last time in Winchester for letters. My family hadn't let me down and neither had Elise. In a quiet spot outside of town I pulled up in the shade to read.

July 10, 1854

Dear William,

Hope this letter finds you well and prospering. Our crops look green and strong with all the rain, but the weeds have flourished as well, so we keep busy with the hoes. Your mother's garden is bountiful and Miranda has finally begun to recognize which plants we eat and which are weeds.

Remember the year the scamp pulled out all the young cabbages? Thomas still maintains she ripped out those shoots because she didn't like the taste, but I'm inclined to forgive her. This year she's helped with the pickles and the jelly. When you make your way north, soon I hope, you'll see what a fine cook she's become. Of course you must praise her highly, or she'll snatch away her samples.

Thomas also fares well. He's taken charge of two fields and his crops are coming in fine, corn and wheat. He's got a farmer's heart, that boy.

We've heard from Lucinda, and she says she's written to you as well. Your mother sniffs the air for romance and smiles a secret smile that makes me jittery. If I must lose a daughter, I confess, I find Jeremiah Strong a fine young man. Quaker or no, I'd welcome him as a son, and hope you'd find him a worthy brother.

The townspeople grow warmer to the Spencer family, a degree at a time. Perhaps they're tired of beating our name into the mud. Your mother says an old story is a cold one, and a tale grows stale with the telling. Perhaps she's right.

Fact is, people are so busy wagging their tongues about the Smith brothers and their troubles, they've had no time for us. The older brother hitched up with a girl from Salem with no notice whatsoever. The biddies surely chew on that. The younger one sold a foul-tempered mare to old Mrs. Baker for her trap. First time she took the beast out, the mare dumped the lady, trap and all, into a ditch. Young Smith didn't make any friends with that sale and had to give the money back. Just deserts, I'd say.

Well, Son, I've just about used up the news. We hope you fare well. Some fellas would have headed home at the first sign of that rainstorm, but you endured. Well done! Your mother calls that spell your baptism and trusts that you will make a success of your new life.

We do wonder if you've encountered any wild birds. We've grown so accustomed to seeing the flocks as they pass by here. We hope you will take the time to further your nature studies as you travel.

We think of you daily and try to imagine where you're journeying and what sights you're seeing. Surely, God's *care will speed you on your way. We commend you to His watchful eye.*

Your loving
Father

Oh, Papa, what a letter. I didn't grieve that those Smith brothers had got their comeuppance or that Papa had fallen to gossip; in fact, I wished he'd written more.

As I scanned the letter again the talk of wild birds made me uneasy. If I'd been living at home, I'd have asked Papa's advice about the coming rescue. Instead, I'd kept it secret, but maybe that was a part of growing up.

And talking about growing up—Mama had sniffed something between Lucy and Jeremiah. Shoot, wouldn't that set the biddies to talking again; a Quaker marrying with a Presbyterian? We went to school with them, and knew them in town, but most folks drew a line. Romance sat on the wrong side of that line. Still, years back, I'd had soft feelings for Charity Strong, Jeremiah's sister, even though she was older.

Soft feelings—I had them now—holding Elise's letter lightly in my hand, saved for last, like you would a sweet slice of plum cake. I'd better write careful in my next letter home. If Mama could sniff out romance, she'd suspect me next, and I wasn't ready for that.

After tucking Papa's pages into the Bible under the wagon seat, I lifted the flap on Elise's letter and slipped the paper out. Did she have soft feelings for me too? With a deep breath, I began to read in the hope I'd find out.

July 15, 1854

Dear Will Spencer,

Your letter brought relief to my heart. With all the rain, I worried you got stuck in mud or washed away by a wild creek and drowned. I do not like the sound of this poison ivy rash, but if you are healed I won't worry.

The rains were bad here, too. Creeks filled, overflowed their banks, gushed into the river. The Ohio rose and washed docks away. A steamboat sank and eleven people drowned, a real tragedy.

Water rose in the warehouses and muddied everything. My uncle and other clothing merchants are having a dreadful time, for their goods are easily spoiled. We pray he will come out of this trouble, but Mama worries. She tosses in the night.

I, too, am restless, but not about Uncle's warehouse. First, I fretted about you and your travels. Your letter made me feel much better, but still I lay awake at night, picturing your face in my mind and wondering, Where is Will now? Who is he meeting? Which farmer shelters him tonight?

I've read your letter over and over. Though safe at home, I have an adventuring spirit and yearn for new people and places. Had I been born a boy, I could find my own adventures, but as a good German daughter, I must count on you for tales and excitement. May I count on you, Will Spencer? Please, write again. And soon.

Your friend,
Elise Schmidt

"Holy smokes, boys," I hooted. "She likes me!"

I jumped down from the wagon seat and shoved the letter right under Sam's nose. He stretched to taste it and I had to yank it away. Still, I plunked a kiss right down on his nose, and one on Charlie's. They tossed their heads like they were real excited.

I read her letter again, this time out loud, so the horses could hear it. The part where she wished she'd been born a boy made me chuckle. Hallelujah—she *wasn't* a boy. Not that I minded pals, but a pal wasn't what I had in mind for Elise. She was too pretty for that.

I sat right down and wrote her another letter, telling about the little towns and distant farms I'd visited and bragging about my nearly empty wagon and full pockets.

The grin on my face nearly broke my jaw, but I couldn't help it. After sealing the letter up, I sprang to my feet with a shout and started turning cartwheels and somersaults. Sam and Charlie tossed their heads like I was some crazy colt who'd lost his mind. More like I'd lost my heart, but I couldn't just sit still. Elise liked me! She did!

A maple tree shaded the clearing, and I reached for a low branch to climb to the sky and shout her name for the world to hear. I jumped and grabbed but missed the branch and landed, sprawling, in the mud. Mood I was in, that didn't even slow me down. But maybe, just maybe, it should have.

Chapter 20

July 18, 1854

Dear Lucy,

Feels like I just landed in the manure pile, everything stinks to high heaven. I'm writing to you, even if this letter never leaves Kentucky—don't have time to wait for an answer anyway; I must act soon. But first I have to get my thoughts reined in, so here goes. If you ever do read this, know that whatever happens, I did the best I could.

Yesterday I headed back toward the Merrick farm, pleased with myself, for my wagon had grown light and my money belt heavy. With luck, in a day or so I'd leave this wretched place behind me, carrying Susannah and an old woman named Delight along.

Well, lo and behold, when I drove up, John Merrick himself sat in a rocking chair on his front porch. Him and another man.

"Been hearing about you, young feller," the stranger said. "Name's Josiah Whitely. Understand you got a wagon and a head for business."

"Yes, sir," I replied.

"My friend John Merrick, here, says you're a fine young man. Straight as an oak tree in your dealings. Haven't cheated a soul in all your travels. That so?"

"Why, yes, sir." My face felt so hot, my cheeks were probably tomatoes.

"How'd you like to do some hauling for me?" Whitely continued. "My wagon broke down and I got a load of merchandise that needs to get to Louisville in a hurry. I'll pay you a fair price, and you can restock your wagon in Louisville."

If I said yes, it would take an extra day or two for me to get Susannah and Miss Delight into Ohio. But nobody would suspect a thing if I was hauling for a Southern man. Besides, with the flood damage in Cincinnati, I might have trouble buying clean goods there, and worse, these men would wonder why I had my mind so set on one town. Then the fella gave me a price.

The amount sounded good, Luce. Too good to be honest. I should have known. But once I hit the river and delivered the goods, turning north would be easy. So

120

I agreed. Gave my word and shook his hand. He paid me twenty dollars right off to seal the bargain. Twenty dollars gold! Then he brought out his cargo.

Oh, Lucy, what I'd done. The man went out to the barn and came back pulling on a chain that had six fellas tied up to it. Fellas young as Tom, who still cried from being ripped away from their families! I'd taken his money to carry six young slaves to a steamboat for selling down the river. Me! I came down here to be a slave stealer but in the blink of an eye, they'd turned me into a soul driver. My stomach sickened, and I had to hold back or else vomit all over my feet.

I ran off, quick. Said I needed to tend to my horses, but I haven't lifted a currycomb yet. All I can do is sit here in misery. Emptied my belly twice, till nothing more would come up, but still my stomach roils and churns.

Lucy, what can I do? If I take the fellas to the riverboat, it will paint sin on my soul forever. But if I don't, I can never show my face here again, never get Susannah and Miss Delight out. I feel like Job in the Bible. First God sent me itches and boils, and now he asks me to betray everything I stand for. Job had patience, but I sure don't. Papa would say pray for help, but God let me get into this fix, and I'm too dang mad to ask Him to help me out.

Aw, Luce, the world's a wicked, wicked place. And now it's making me turn wicked too. What am I going to do?

William

121

Dang it. My mind was so riled up, I'd written to Lucy in plain words, without hiding a thing. I tore up the page and threw the pieces into a prickly bramble patch that edged the pasture, then set about grooming my horses. That was the one thing I could do that didn't hurt anybody. I was still working at it when the two men came back to check my wagon.

"Nice-built wagon," Josiah Whitely began. "Sturdy frame and good, wide wheels."

"Like I told you," John Merrick said. "He's a good boy. Honest as the day. Takes care of his team right well, too." He scratched Charlie's nose, and I wished for a moment that Charlie was a mean horse and would bite the man's hand.

Josiah Whitely patted Sam's rump, then turned to me. "We got ourselves a deal, son. We start traveling tomorrow, soon as it's light."

"Yes, sir." My mind scrambled for an escape but found nothing.

The ugly man went on talking. "My friend John, here, he'll sell me food for the boys; you'll do the cooking. And we won't travel too hard, nor rough them up. I want them clean and unmarked. Right healthy when they arrive in New Orleans. You got a problem with any of that? You ain't in a hurry, are you?"

"Um, no. No problem, no hurry. And I drive real careful, too." Chewing my bottom lip, I wondered how to get out of this. If I wedged a stone under one of my horse's feet, he'd come up lame, but horses were plentiful. This

122

man would just hire another team for my wagon. He'd said one thing I might be able to use, though. "Mr. Whitely, sir . . . ?"

"What is it, boy? You want more money? I paid you a good fare; you get the rest when the job's done."

"It's not money, sir. It's the food. I can't cook worth spit. So unless you do the cooking . . ."

"Land sakes, I ain't no cook. Beans and corn bread will do, boy. I just don't want them looking skinny at the auction. John, here, he could sell us cooked dinners instead of just fixin's."

"I don't know, sir. Already-cooked food . . . It could go bad in a day or two and we'd all be sick—puking."

He scowled at me. "It don't have to taste good, just fill them up. What do you feed on when you're traveling?"

"I trade, sir. Chores for a meal. I'm real sorry, but I burn most everything. You'd rather eat a rock."

"Dang it, John. You said he was the answer to my troubles. I can't have me and them boys starved to death. They won't bring enough to pay for their keep."

"Now, Josiah, give me a minute. I'll think of something," Merrick said.

Don't, please don't, I prayed silently, but again, God didn't care much about my opinions.

"I got it!" Merrick slapped his leg. "That useless old woman. Delight Webber. Take her with you, boy. She'll cook for you on the road. That's about all she's up to these days, cooking and watching the babies. Tell you what, Josiah, you sell her off in the market and give me a

123

share next time you pass through. She's been acting up and the wife's plumb tired of trying to keep her in line. Been hammering at me to get rid of that old gal. Yessir, this solves a problem for you and a problem for me. How about it?"

No, not Miss Delight too! I couldn't bear it.

Josiah Whitely slapped John Merrick on the back and they walked off, joking over the good deal they'd made. I just stood there numb. Now I had to betray not six but seven people, and one of them was an old woman who had been kind to me. Where would this ever end?

Chapter 21

Arms aching, I finally had to stop brushing Charlie and Sam and return to Miss Delight's cabin. When I couldn't put it off another minute, I trudged back, keeping my eyes on the ground and avoiding the angry faces that watched me. Near the row of cabins, silence followed me like a tracking hound.

When I knocked at Miss Delight's door, Susannah opened it and let me in, but her eyes shot me through with hate. I couldn't much blame her.

Miss Delight sat on her bench, her hands folded. "Dear Lord, you brought folks out of Egypt with your man Moses. We be your folks too. Show us a way, Lord. Lead us to your promised land."

I sat down at her feet. "Ma'am, those fellas. I don't know what to do. I've thought and thought but nothing comes."

"Hush up and let me pray."

"I won't stay in the same house with him," Susannah said. She hurried toward the door.

"Ssst! I said hush. Put food on the table, gal. Haul in your temper. If we ever need clear heads, it be this night."

Susannah did what Miss Delight said, but she kept shooting ugly looks at me. Well, fine.

"You know, Susannah . . . ," I began softly.

She turned so her back was all I could see, stiff and unbending.

"Fine. Don't look at me. But I'll say my piece and you'll hear it if I have to yell to kingdom come. Part of this misery is your durned fault. If you'd come north when I first got here, we'd be long gone. I wouldn't have to carry no fellas."

She spun around, her eyes wild. "And James? I was supposed to leave without knowing about my brother?"

"He left, durn it. Went off without you. He'd want you to get free. I do, and I'm not your brother. I want it for those fellas, and I don't even know them." I kicked at the stones of the fireplace and got my boot all sooty.

She wiped her face like she was crying or close to it. I ought to have comforted her, but I felt more like punching something.

"You really want them boys to make free?" Miss Delight asked.

"Yes, ma'am. I came here for James, but I'd find a

hundred Jameses in this old Kentucky and haul them all north if I could."

"We do it, then," she said.

"What, steal them right out from under Josiah Whitely's nose? How are we going to do that?"

"Let me think some," she said.

I shook my head at her. "Miss Delight, even if I could carry you and the fellas north, what would happen to Susannah? If somehow we pry those fellas loose, I better never show my face in these parts again. How will Susannah get free?"

"I ain't worth worrying about." Susannah's voice was low and pained. "Six boys and Miss Delight. One of me. Take 'em north, William. Leave me here. You right. If I go when you first come . . ." She started to cry.

Her crying made me want to head for the woods. "Dang it, Susannah. It's not just your fault. If I'd hurried, James might not have run. I poked along in Cincinnati and then rested up four whole days after that rain quit. I'm just as much to blame. . . ."

"No blaming," Miss Delight ordered. "We got to think and plan. Talk real quiet, you never know who's outside."

Nobody spoke. Muffled footsteps sounded in the distance.

I paced, waiting, then whispered, "Let's take one thing at a time. First, how can we get rid of that ugly slave dealer?"

Miss Delight tilted her head to the side. "Tonight I might just take a little walk, back into the hills. Could be I'll find me some roots and leaves."

"You'd poison the soul driver?" Susannah asked.

"Not permanent," the old woman said. "But once we let him carry us away from this place, I'd slow him down some."

"And how will we find a safe route out with all those fellas?" I asked. "If we do like you say and let Josiah Whitely start the trip, we'll travel too far from Winchester and I won't know the route north, or the river crossings."

"Could be I'll run into Ezekiel in the woods," she said. "He got pictures in his head—every road, every hill, every creek."

"We could use that." I caught sight of Susannah's face. Her eyes looked like they'd spill over any moment. "Miss Delight, what about Susannah? If we sneak her out with us, John Merritt is sure to follow within hours. If we get away without her, then how—"

"Ezekiel," she said. "He been helping folks north a long time. He start her on the right path. We meet up later. You willing to go by yourself, gal?"

Susannah shrugged. "Guess so. Got no other choice."

"But old John Merrick," I began. "Even if she goes off by herself, he'll come right after. He'll find her and she'll get in trouble and the fellas will get caught. He thinks . . . we like each other."

"I can fix that easy," Susannah said. She stood a little straighter and lifted her chin. "I can fuss at you so bad, you never want to come back for me. You ain't the only one carrying a fire inside."

"Wouldn't be the first time Susa whup somebody with her tongue," Miss Delight said. "But at least we can feed you first."

I ate without saying much, too weighed down by worry to even notice what I was putting in my mouth.

When the meal was gone, Susannah unleashed her tongue. "I sick a you! You git out, you ugly peddler boy! You think pretty ribbons make me soft! I ain't lying with no soul driver! You don't own me, you can't make me!"

I had to say something, pretend a fight. It wasn't all that hard, for my mind was filled up with trouble and I'd just got the scorching of my life. "If you ain't the stubbornnest girl I ever met . . ."

"Get out and take your calico and your lace with you! I wouldn't dress a hog in them! Get!"

"I'm getting and never coming back! I'm sick of you, too! I can find lots prettier girls, and sweeter ones."

I grabbed my hat and slammed out of the cabin. From a darkened window someone chuckled and a voice said, "Good for you, Susa."

As I marched toward my wagon, I hoped the voice was right—that what we were doing *would* be good for Susannah—and for me and Miss Delight and all those chained-up fellas.

But the way luck was falling around here, I didn't have much faith we'd succeed. In the cool night air, with my mind awake and sensible, I figured our chances were as flimsy as a snip of that lace I sold to farm wives. But we had to try; it was our only choice.

Chapter 22

I never felt so low down in my life as when Josiah
Whitely led his string of fellas out of the barn and
dragged them up to my wagon. People from the cabins
watched in silence as the iron chains clanked. Their eyes
smoked at me, like punk wood that won't burn but just
smolders. Hate hovered in the air, invisible, with no
smell or taste, but so strong, I could nearly touch it. It
weighed down the wagon as the fellas climbed up. It
landed on my shoulders, making me heavy inside, so I
could barely breathe.

Miss Delight and the woman called Bess loaded the
wagon with a basket of breakfast leavings, sacks of

cornmeal and beans, and some old pots and gear. Then Miss Delight lifted herself into the back with the fellas.

"Wait," I began.

She glared and I bit back the words. I'd been careless, expecting her to sit on the wagon seat with me. I wasn't supposed to treat Miss Delight like a regular person.

"What is it, boy?" Josiah Whitely asked. He climbed on the back of his horse and edged closer to the wagon.

"Um . . . water. More water," I said. "Just in case."

John Merrick sent a couple of young girls for buckets, and they filled a barrel on the side of my wagon, glaring at me like I was the worst person on earth. Well, I was, just then.

Once the water was loaded and the barrel capped, Josiah Whitely nodded to me and nudged his horse. I called to my team and followed. Up the lane, Susannah stood silent and stern, but she'd folded her hands at her waist and I took heart. She'd tied cloth there beneath her dress and hidden money in it, money I'd given her for food and a ferry ride if our plans went bad and we didn't meet up.

When we got to the end of the lane, we turned westward on the rutted road. The fellas in the back of the wagon started in crying and moaning. Miss Delight hushed them some, but the sound cut me deep inside, and I had to grind my teeth to keep from hollering out.

"Forgive me. Forgive me for all this," I muttered to myself. An hour later, my ears were sore from all the cries of

131

"Mama, Mama," and from all the sobs of "No, no, sweet Jesus."

I glanced back over my shoulder. "Miss Delight . . ."

"What?"

"Did you get what we need?"

"Didn't sleep last night, if that's what you worrying about."

"But the—"

"Ssst! Can't talk now," she whispered. "Later."

It wasn't until we stopped for our noon meal that I got a chance to talk with her alone. Josiah Whitely took the fellas off into the trees to relieve themselves, and I helped her set out cooked bacon, boiled eggs, and cold johnnycakes.

"Did you find those plants?"

"Got me two or three roots I can mash up and put in his food."

"Won't poison him, will it? That would get us in worse trouble." Bad as he was, I couldn't live with a man's death on my soul.

"His belly gonna cramp up pretty bad. Slow him down a day or two, that be enough?"

"It'll have to be. Did you meet up with Mister Ezekiel?"

She stuck her hand in her pocket and passed me a folded-up paper. "Here. He make a picture with roads and where to cross over. Other parts he tell and I save up in my mind."

I unfolded the paper, but Miss Delight nudged my hand. "Ssst. They coming back now. Put that away. No more talking."

I jammed the paper into my shirt as the fellas shuffled back to the wagon in a ragged line. The small one at the end had to hobble to keep up, and I heard the ugly sound of iron clanking as they moved. Durn chains. Josiah Whitely strolled along, smiling like he didn't have a care in the world. I caught myself hoping that the roots Miss Delight had found would make him heave up his toenails.

That paper from Mister Ezekiel itched at me all afternoon. I wanted to study it but didn't dare, for Whitely rode his fancy bay stallion right next to the wagon seat. To spare me from eating his dust, he said, but I figured he just wanted to keep a close eye on his property. So until he was taken care of, the paper would have to stay folded up.

I'd have felt a lot better if this were happening in Ohio, up near Atwater, where I knew my way around, instead of in these durn Kentucky hills. But at least we had something like a map.

We rode west all that day, and by suppertime the sun blazed in my eyes and even my hat didn't help. I recognized the road, though, for Mister Ezekiel and I had traveled it from the Harlow farm.

Finally Whitely pulled up his horse and pointed. "There's a creek and a clearing not far. See that track. We'll camp back in there for the night."

"Fine. Horses could use a good drink," I said.

We pulled into a clearing where old stones marked the remains of a burnt-out house. Again, Whitely took charge of the fellas, unloading them from the wagon and taking them up the creek.

Miss Delight stood close to me while I unhitched my team. "Ezekiel, he say we got to make the soul driver sick this night. Be a farm nearby, he might rest up. Say you'd know where this farm be."

"Harlow's. Yep, I can find it. How sick's he gonna get?"

"His belly gonna turn inside out, upside down. Fever too. Won't kill him, but he won't forget it neither. You gotta be the one takes him to the farm. I'm not supposed to know about it."

"Sure, that makes sense. How will you get the roots into his food without making the rest of us sick?"

"I got ways. You take care your horses. I take care of this."

"But Miss Delight . . ."

She shook her head. "You don't know what gonna happen, you can't give nothin' away. Now don't act nice to me or these younguns. You working for the soul driver, you got to be his best friend tonight. Otherwise . . ."

She stopped talking as iron chains clanked and the soul driver led six sad fellas back to the clearing. When I looked at their faces and imagined being his best friend, my stomach twisted. I wondered how I'd get through the evening without losing my supper, roots or no.

Miss Delight cooked up beans and salt pork, and by the time the food was ready, I was hungry again, in spite of the night's work ahead of us. "I chop up some wild onion on the beans," she said as she served Whitely and me. "Give some flavor."

"Thanks." I figured what she really meant was the wild onion would hide some other flavors. "I'm partial to onions."

"Yep," Whitely said. He dug into his plate of beans like he hadn't been fed for a week. He asked for seconds, too, and ate that plateful like the hungry dog that he was. I ate my first helping, but once the edge was off my appetite, I just sat back and dug a stick into the dry dirt by my boot. Across the clearing, Miss Delight and the fellas sat and ate without much talking.

When Whitely finished, he pulled a bottle from his pocket and uncorked it. He held the bottle to his lips and swallowed some down, then wiped off the rim. "Like a nip?"

I frowned. If Mama or Papa suspected I'd tried hard liquor, grown or not, I'd get a hiding. But Miss Delight had told me to be this man's best friend tonight.

I took the bottle from his hand and wiped it again, hoping that whatever she'd put in his food was long gone and wouldn't get into my stomach. A single sip made my throat close up, and I choked and spat it out.

He laughed. "Nothing but a green boy, are you? Never tasted white lightning before?"

White lightning? Two barrels of the danged stuff sat in the wagon. I wiped my mouth and scraped my tongue with my teeth. "That tastes worse than when Mama doses us for the grippe. How come you drink it?"

"Once you get over the taste, it ain't bad. Good old corn whiskey—gives you a nice warm feeling inside. Here, have some more."

"No thanks. I ain't over the taste yet."

He laughed again. "How long you been hauling, boy? Big as you are, you don't seem quite growed."

I couldn't find anything wrong with telling the truth, so I did. "This is my first trip, sir. Sold all my goods, too, so maybe I'll stick to hauling for a while. Buying and selling. Pile up some cash money."

"Not a bad plan." He leaned closer and spoke in a quiet voice. "You want to pile up cash money faster, you might think about my kind of hauling. Like you said, buying and selling. Profits are real sweet on my cargo." He nodded over to where Miss Delight and the fellas sat.

My throat closed up again. I snapped the stick I'd been fiddling with into pieces and just shrugged.

"Yes, sir," he went on. "A man can make real good money buying and selling. Unless, being from the North, he's got himself a problem with certain goods." He studied me, and I was glad it was evening and the light was getting dim.

"Don't know as I'd have a problem," I finally managed to say. "Just never thought about it before, being from the North, like you say. We don't have that kind of trade up where I come from."

"Would you be interested? You got yourself a fine wagon. Working together, we could cover more territory."

My mind screamed at me and I bit back the words. *I'd be interested in seeing you chained up, Mr. Josiah Whitely. Interested in watching you get whipped, or lose a finger or toe. Interested in stealing all your cargo from now till kingdom come and hauling them up to Canada.* But I couldn't say a word of that, just patted my stomach where Mister Ezekiel's paper was hidden.

I said the first thing I dared, even if it was as far from truth as noon from midnight. "How much would it cost me to get started? Made good money on this trip, but it probably ain't enough."

"Me, I started small." He sipped at his whiskey. "You could pick up a youngun for a few hundred dollars, sell him, and make a couple hundred. I clear between one-fifty and two hundred a head, after food and expenses. Course, I get the best prices with all my connections—river captains, the right times to go to auction, good farms for buying stock. If you was to work with me, son, you'd get in on all that. Start with a small stake and watch it grow. Are you interested?"

My hands fisted up and I pounded them together. For tonight, I'd have to play along with his game, no matter how ugly it made me feel. I glanced across the clearing, hoping that Miss Delight and the fellas were too far away to hear me.

"Tell you what, Mr. Whitely. I'll think on it. Try it out on this trip and see how it fits. We could talk again when we get to the river."

"Now, that's a smart boy. You ain't jumping into the

creek right off, but you ain't afraid of the water, neither. You and me, we're going to get on fine." He stuck out his hand and I shook it, wondering just how long it would take for Miss Delight's roots to start working in his belly. I was plenty sick to my stomach already.

Chapter 23

When his moans started, I was lying on my bedroll, counting stars. Whitely was asleep, for he'd drunk enough whiskey to put a horse under and didn't wake up right away, but he thumped around and kicked off his blankets. Then I heard retching noises.

When it got loud enough that it would wake a heavy sleeper, I sat up and tried to sound dumb and sleepy. "Hey, Mr. Whitely. You having a bad dream?"

"Dang it, boy." He coughed and retched again.

A sour smell drifted over toward me. I had to hurry off into the bushes to get away from that stench and relieve myself. When I got back, he sounded like he'd quit for a while.

"Mr. Whitely, you sick?"

"As a dog," he said. "Too much whiskey. A man pays for his pleasures."

"Can I get you anything, sir? A drink of water?"

"That would be right nice. Got a tin cup here."

He passed me his cup and I went to the creek. Him being sick didn't do much for my digestion, so I splashed cool water on my face and took a batch of deep breaths before filling the cup and carrying it back. Then I remembered what Mama said when one of us got sick.

"Sip it slow, now. Your stomach's tender, you don't want to upset it any more."

"Now, ain't you the mother hen? Big old boy like you." He laughed and I felt like a fool, but acting a fool was better than having him figure out what we were up to. I stood and dragged my bedroll out of range.

"Mr. Whitely, I got a weak stomach. Hope you don't mind if I move away a bit. I'll still be here if you need me, just call out."

"Do what you like, boy. I'll sleep like the angels for the rest of the night. See you in the morning."

Well, he saw me three more times that night, for he kept getting sick and I kept toting water for him. When morning finally came and I could see his face, he looked green as a frog.

Miss Delight and the fellas made breakfast while I hitched up. I got me a plate and talked real loud to Miss Delight while I ate. "He was sick in the night," I explained. "We might have to stay here a couple of days. We could run low on food, so maybe you'd want to make small meals today. That won't hurt the young fellas, will it?"

"You there, Will. Get over here."

I crossed the clearing. "Yes, sir, Mr. Whitely."

"What you talking to her for?"

I repeated my words, holding my plate where he'd be sure to smell my breakfast. He turned even greener and went off behind a tree.

When he came back, he scowled at me. "Get that food out of my sight. Can't you see it's making me sick? Now let's get loaded up; we got miles to cover today."

"Is that a good idea, you being sick and all?"

"Like you said, if we don't keep moving, we'll run low on food. Can't have that. Plus, I got a steamboat to meet. Gets into Louisville in six days. These fellas need to be on that boat."

"But you're sick."

"It was just whiskey. I'll mend. What I need is some coffee."

I brought him a cup and of course it made him sick again. Seemed like the right time to stir things up. "You know, Mr. Whitely, I had the grippe about a week ago. Felt real bad for two or three days. All I wanted was to lie still and sleep. Maybe you got the same thing. Might want to rest here until you're better."

"Your ears plugged up, boy? Didn't you hear me say I got a boat to meet?"

"Just hope you'll be all right. Want to ride in the wagon? We can tie your horse behind."

"Good idea. Thank you, son. You been tending me real nice."

I stayed nice as long as it took to lay out his bedroll and settle him into the wagon. Then I remembered how terrible the fellas' moans had sounded the day before. I whispered to Miss Delight and she nodded and whispered back. When I took the fellas off to the bushes before loading up, I repeated what she'd told me to say, plenty loud.

"Now see here. We're going to make a lot of miles today. That man, he's gonna get you to Louisville and in six days you're gonna be riding a boat to New Orleans. So say goodbye to everything you knew before, cause you ain't never coming back here again."

Saying it made me feel like a low-down cur, but in part it was true. However this turned out, if they went with Whitely, or if we stole them up to Canada, they'd have a new life. Well, my words did for their hearts like Miss Delight's roots did for Whitely's stomach, and they started in crying so loud I thought my ears would pop.

As we headed off on the day's journey, I got a notion that a rough ride would upset Mr. Whitely, so I searched out the ruts and bumps in the road. The hollering of the fellas added to the poor driving and made Charlie and Sam nervous, so they weren't pulling smooth, like they usually do. My rump got plenty sore on the wagon seat.

The more Whitely yelled for the fellas to be quiet and let him sleep, the louder they cried. I had to stop the wagon twice in the first hour, so he could get out and empty his stomach. Each time, I hollered at the fellas to quiet down and cuffed them around the shoulders to show Whitely I meant business.

After he'd heaved the second time, it seemed like he might just be miserable enough to listen to reason. I stood next to him in the shade of an oak tree.

"Mr. Whitely, sir. Have you got a fever?"

"I might. Did you have one when you got that grippe?"

"Sure did. Hot one minute, cold the next. And trembling."

"I felt some of that. How long did you say it lasted?"

I made it sound bad. "I was out of my head part of the time; don't remember exactly how long. Two or three days. And I couldn't quit vomiting. Wore me right out. You know, I've been thinking. We ain't making very good time, with all the stops. Not that I'm blaming you or anything."

"Go on."

"Well, there's a farm up the road. Folks sheltered me and dried me out after that rainy spell. You might want to rest there, where it's quiet and the ride won't jolt you. I'd make better time without all the stops and you could meet me in Louisville. Once you're feeling yourself, you'll cover more miles riding that horse than I will with a full wagon."

"It's an idea. Folks who own that farm, they're decent?"

"Plenty nice to me."

"I'll think on it. Suppose I could risk a drink? I'm parched."

"Lets get you back to the wagon first, and I'll fill your cup."

What with the bumping and the moaning and two more stops to be sick, old Josiah Whitely was ready to spend a day or two in the Harlows' stable loft. Mrs. Harlow insisted on feeding me, while Miss Delight dished up some leftover beans for the fellas.

When we'd eaten, I spoke again, like any hauler would. "I'll carry these fellas real careful, Mr. Whitely."

He shook his head at me and frowned. "It's a mighty full load for a young man's first trip. I just don't know if this is the right thing to do."

I almost laughed in his face. What this durned fool didn't know, what he couldn't even imagine, was that I'd hauled more folks than this, and not just once, either. But I intended to keep that a complete secret.

Instead of laughing, I pasted a big old scowl on my face. "Are you saying you don't trust me, Whitely?" I reached into my trouser pocket, yanked out a leather pouch, and untied the strings. "You can just keep your dang money and haul these bawling boys yourself. I was doing you a favor, but—"

"Slow down, Will. I ain't myself and that's a fact. A man empties his gullet as much as I have, he don't always think straight. You'll do a good job for me. This here farmer vouches for you. And even though you're young, you're plenty big."

I kept scowling at him for a minute, just to make him stew. Then I jammed that leather pouch back in my pocket. "All right, then. Where shall we meet in Louisville?"

"There's a big dock in town, right on the riverfront. Be there in six days. Boat you're looking for, she's the *Mary Bee*. If I don't catch up, set these boys aboard. Captain Burford will take care of things for me." Whitely scrawled out a letter saying I had permission to haul his goods and that the captain should take them on board.

I stuck his letter inside my shirt right next to the map. Then I yanked on that mean-looking chain and hauled the youngsters back into the wagon as rough as I could. "Git, you," I hollered. "I'm the boss man now. You'll do as I say or else be sorry."

"Captain Burford and the *Mary Bee*, don't forget," Whitely said.

I nodded to him and grinned as if I was enjoying all this. I'd remember, all right, and stay as far from that man and boat as a person could. "You rest up until you feel better, sir."

"I will, son. You're a good boy." He shook my hand. His hand was weak and dry and hot.

I felt terrible then, for he trusted me with his business and I was planning to steal him blind. He'd even called me son. That was hard to swallow, for he was nothing like Papa.

I didn't like making friends with people who owned slaves or sold them. Made me wonder what kind of fella I was if such wicked people liked me. It was a puzzle, but puzzle or no, I had a wagon, a cargo, and a fair day for traveling, so I set off and tried to leave my itchy conscience behind.

Chapter 24

We needed distance between us and Josiah Whitely, so I pushed Charlie and Sam hard that afternoon. A mile past the Harlow farm, I pulled out Mister Ezekiel's map. It showed the road we were traveling and a track ahead that would take us straight north. He'd marked spots where we could camp for the night if the time worked out right. And he'd drawn Susannah's route, which was different from ours, for it took creek beds and back trails.

Miss Delight rode next to me on the wagon seat and spoke quiet. She told me about a river crossing near Ripley, Ohio, and a place called the Freedom Steps. I traced our route over and over, until it stuck firm in my mind. We'd burn the paper when we stopped for supper that night.

She'd calmed the fellas, and they didn't make such a ruckus as before. I wondered about it. "Did you tell them we were going north instead of south? Is that why they stopped crying?"

"Not yet. Just said rest and save up strength, so they don't get sick like that soul dealer. He got pretty nasty." She smiled.

"Roots worked fine. Can we tell them now? I'll break off their chains."

"What you got in your head where the brains supposed to be?"

"What do you mean? Why can't I take the chains off?"

"Think, peddler boy. Pretend you eleven or twelve, snatched away from home and mama. Somebody break off the chain, what you gonna do?"

"Well, I'd . . ." Her questions stopped me. Sure I was opposed to slavery, but hadn't really imagined myself wearing chains. I scowled. If I was one of them fellas, stolen away, then set loose . . . "I'd run for home like hornets were chasing me."

She nodded. "Suppose even one run for home. What then?"

She was leading me someplace, but I wasn't sure where. If one or two fellas went back where they'd come from . . . Of course. They'd been sold, so if they went back, folks would know something had gone wrong.

147

People would come after us and we'd all get caught. Didn't bear thinking about.

"Sorry, ma'am. When can we break off those terrible chains?"

"I don't know," she said. "We got to get far enough they can't find home. Ssst now, no more talking and no acting soft. Remember, you carrying me off to get sold. Far as they know"—she raised her voice so even the squirrels could hear—"you my enemy too, you worthless soul driver."

Enemy. Worthless. Soul driver. The words burned in my ears, and I felt eyes on my back as I drove. There were six of them and only one of me. If I was them, I'd grab the worthless soul driver, dump him off the wagon, and leave him behind in the woods. I sure hoped they didn't take such a notion. I rode through the long day perched on the wagon seat like it was covered with tacks, looking over my shoulder at the slightest sound.

Miss Delight didn't talk to me again until dusk came down and we stopped. Then I asked her if we could break the chains soon.

"These boys been slaves they whole life," she said. "One or two more days, it ain't nothin'."

"Bad enough playing soul driver while Josiah Whitely was along," I grumbled. "I can't do this much longer."

"All of us do what we got to. God send you down here to deliver us, he won't give you up. You need strength, just pray. Trouble come, he send down his angel to watch over us. Don't you know that yet?"

Her words shamed me, and I vowed to try harder and endure.

Next day, rains came. Miss Delight sat in the back of the wagon and stitched, making shirts and trousers for the journey north from my last pieces of cloth. The fellas cried on and off, and what with the rain and mud and crying, the riding went on forever.

We rode like that for two miserable damp days. Kentucky seemed like the most waterlogged place in creation. Of course, my patience had all but worn away. I'd gotten used to being alone, but being alone in a wagon filled with people was strange. I felt like I had a sickness and they'd put me under quarantine. All I could think to cheer myself was that we'd gotten away from Whitely. With luck, Susannah had run by now. But it was cold comfort, for if she'd run, she was in danger.

Sure, I'd done this kind of work in Ohio, but there was more than a river separating my Ohio from this wretched Kentucky. I couldn't count the number of ways I didn't belong here. And I couldn't get home to Ohio and freedom soon enough.

On the third day, the sun finally showed his face, and by then we were riding straight north on a rough, overgrown track toward the river and the town of Ripley. In the back of the wagon the fellas dozed off and on.

I'd been acting and talking mean for miles, but Miss Delight wouldn't let me quit, not yet. "You got them shirts done, old woman?" I growled as the afternoon wore on and we came near to a piney woods along a noisy creek.

149

"Finished, every one. Pantaloons, too. I ain't forgot how to stitch."

"Don't go forgetting how to cook, neither," I ordered, then lowered my voice to a whisper. "Can you make up a big batch of beans and corn bread, Miss Delight? After tonight we won't be able to risk a fire, nor open travel, and we'll need another couple days of careful riding to get across."

"I'll cook as much as we can carry," she whispered back. "Is that a creek I hear? You get these younguns clean while I start the fire."

"Yes, ma'am."

I pulled up the horses and climbed down, leading them farther into the pines. I woke the fellas and hustled them down from the wagon toward a place where the creek widened out into a nice pool. With the sun hot and sweat stinging my eyes, it looked like heaven, so I plunged right in and ducked my head under. Cool water, and clean.

"No! No!" Somebody tugged on the chain and hollered.

"What's the matter?" I barked at the fella closest to me.

He shrugged. "Don't know, suh. Don't know him much."

A couple of the fellas nearest me ducked down to splash and take drinks. I made my way to the one who hollered.

"What's wrong?"

"Don't pull me in. Don't!"

"What? Can't you swim?"

He shook his head. "You gonna drown me?"

"What?"

"I been crying. You get tired of me. I see it in your face."

"Yeah. I'm tired of the crying. Tired of hauling all of you too. Look, get yourself clean by this rock. It ain't deep here." I turned back and dove under again, but as fresh as the water was, it couldn't wash away my dirty feelings. We'd come far enough; I had to do something about that now.

The fellas trudged up the bank to the wagon, dripping and clanking. Miss Delight had a fire going. "You all look a sight better," she said.

I stood close and spoke in a careful voice. "Miss Delight, please. Tell these fellas what we've planned."

"How far we come?" She stirred beans into a pot.

"Fifty miles, maybe more. We've got to get the chains off soon so they can hide under the floorboards of my wagon, and unless they understand what we're planning, one of them will run for sure."

"All right." She turned to the fellas. "You boys. Set yourselves here close by the fire. We got some talking to do."

As Miss Delight began to speak, I rummaged in my toolbox for a chisel and sledge to break open the heavy iron chains that were fastened to rings around their ankles.

"This peddler boy, he come lookin' for a gal called Susa and her brother James. James be about your size." She pointed to a medium-sized fella, who stared at me with a big scowl on his face. "James run off afore this peddler boy come, so the peddler fixing to take Susa and me up north, where they don't make folks slaves."

The fellas started to talk, buzzing among themselves. "When he agree to haul goods for that soul driver, he think he be hauling barley, not boys," she went on. They stopped talking to listen. "He ain't no slaver."

I knelt down next to the small fella, the one who'd been afraid I'd drown him. He backed away with a scared look on his face.

"Please. Let me pound the chains off."

He still held back, but one at the other end of the line called out, "Cut my chain, then. Mine first." His voice sounded angry.

"Wait," Miss Delight said. She turned to the one who wanted to be first. "Your mama teach you to listen to a old woman?"

"Yes, ma'am."

"Good. Listen hard. You want to run off, fine. But you run back where you come from, they just sell you all over again. Except they might chop off a toe or two first. You hear me? Them cotton fields hungry for boys."

"Yes, ma'am. But—"

"Don't give me no buts. You do as I say or you keep wearing that iron." She glared at him until he blinked and looked down at the dirt.

"Talk to them, peddler."

I stood still and held in my breath. There was so much to say, and they had so little reason to listen.

I sat down and started to work on the first chain, looking for a weak link or one that was already spreading apart. "Look, you fellas," I began. "You ever do any pretending? Ever play like you were somebody else?"

A couple of them looked puzzled and shook their heads. The one who had talked back to Miss Delight stared at me for a minute. Then he spoke. "Back in the cabins I play at being the Master. I tell everybody what to do. Say I'll whup them if they don't listen."

"And you're not really the Master, are you?"

"You crazy?"

"Probably," I admitted. "But just like you're not the Master, I'm not a soul dealer. I've been pretending. I hate slavery and want to get you free."

With a deep breath, I started hammering away at the thick iron chain. "My name is Will Spencer. I come from a little town called Atwater, Ohio, and I bought this wagon to haul goods. But lately, I've been hauling more people than goods. . . ."

I didn't know if they believed me or not, but I just hammered and talked till my throat got dry. Told them about Lucy, about Tom and Miranda, and all the animals they found and took care of. Told them about how Mama and Papa had started us on the Railroad and about Canada and how they could live free there. I must have done all right, for when my story ran out, nobody left. Miss Delight fed us and set more food to cook, for the days to come.

When she sent the fellas off to wash the bowls in the

creek, I sat back down beside the fire. I'd put away my chisel and sledge, but those durned chains still lay in the dirt. I prodded them with my toe. If we heard riders coming, Miss Delight and I could make it seem like the fellas were still captive. But once they started riding under the floorboards, no amount of iron would make me look like anything other than a slave stealer.

I lifted a chain and studied it. Heavy. Cold. I tried to imagine being dragged around, one leg hobbled. It sent chills up my back. I dropped the chain with a loud, metallic clunk. That decided it. If I carried the blasted things in my wagon and we hit a rut, they'd make such a racket, we'd get caught for sure.

As I headed to the wagon for a shovel, another worry climbed up on my shoulder. Most of the fellas still wore a link or two, for the iron ankle bands had been too tight to pound off. That metal would jangle. I pulled out a shovel and grabbed cloth scraps left over from Miss Delight's stitching.

"Ma'am?"

"What you need? Some patching done? I get my needle."

"No, it's the noise. I'll bury the chains. Could you help the fellas wrap cloth around the iron they're still wearing? For quiet when we ride."

"You got a smart head on you shoulders this day," she said. "I'll see to it. Thank you." She put her warm hand on my arm for a moment and it felt like a blessing.

For once, I'd done something right.

154

Chapter 25

A s the evening light faded, the fellas wrapped their ankles in dark blue strips. I lifted a couple of floorboards in the wagon and showed them the hiding place, and the notches under the seat where I kept track of how many folks I'd hauled north. Then the questions started.

"How we all gonna fit in there?"

"Can I try it out?"

"You'll fit," I said. "I've carried eight before."

"When you put the boards back, won't it get real dark?"

I heard fear in that voice. "No darker than regular night. And you'll be together, for comfort."

"You gonna cut marks for us?" the smallest asked,

running his hand over the marks I'd made during the past several years.

"You bet. When we meet up in Canada, we'll have a big old party. You can cut your own notches."

Night came down like a dark cloud and still nobody sneaked off. I couldn't sleep, for thinking about Susannah. As the stars showed I counted them, watching for the North Star. The fellas could follow that star if something bad happened or we got separated. But durn, I hated to imagine such things. They were young to travel alone. Then again, so was she. I sat there a long time and the moon rose up; only a thin sliver showed. There was light, but not too much.

Miss Delight had been fussing with food at the fire, and she walked over to me. "Get you some sleep."

"Miss Delight, what about Susannah?"

"She in God's hands. And Ezekiel's."

"What if she changed her mind? What if she stays to wait for James?"

"James in God's hands too. Susa be coming. You get some rest."

She made it sound so easy, but it wasn't, not for me. "Can't sleep, ma'am. Got to stay awake and watch out for things."

One of the fellas might run; Susannah might get lost, or worse, be followed. And we were deep in Kentucky, breaking the law. It was night and I didn't much trust the critters, human or wild, who hunted at night, so I sat as the slice of moon crept higher and the air grew cool.

156

The next time I opened my eyes the sky had lightened to gray. Leaves rustled nearby. I turned and looked into the face of a young doe with the prettiest brown eyes. I held still and tried not to scare her. She sniffed, blinked, then ambled away to sample some tall grass by my wagon. She grazed as the sky went from gray to pearl. Then noises came from the wagon and she flicked her tail and ran for cover.

The fellas were awake and moving about. One of the older ones shook his leg, which still rattled. He bent to rewrap the iron. "Didn't dream it. How about that? He really did chop off them chains. Maybe he will take us up north, like the old one say."

They filed out of the wagon and headed for the creek. I watched them go, their faces still puffy from sleep but their eyes watchful. They were more cautious about me than the doe had been, but I couldn't blame them. "Good morning," I said, smiling sweet as if I was talking to church ladies.

By the time they straggled back, Miss Delight was up. She passed each boy a set of new clothes she'd been stitching on since we'd left old Whitely behind. Then she served bowls of cold beans and corn bread. She wore a frown and had deep shadows under her eyes. She'd slept poorly, too.

"You think maybe we should look for Susannah?" I asked.

"No. Lord only know if she ahead or behind, this road or that. We best keep moving; that man ain't gonna stay

157

sick forever. My mind already travel to freedom. These old bones want to go too."

"You think we've got enough food?"

"We'll do." She pointed to the sky. "Clouds coming. Best load the wagon afore they open up and soak everything."

Just what we needed, more danged rain. I began to shift the goods out of the wagon.

"What you doing?" the smallest fella asked.

"Getting ready," I explained. "When you were chained, you could ride in the open. People would think I was taking you to the steamboat. Now you got to hide. Remember, I showed you last night."

"You really carry us away from here?"

"Yep. Want to give me a hand with that barrel?"

They pitched in and soon we had the goods on the ground and all the floorboards opened up. "This wagon was built special, like I told you. You'll ride bumpy but safe. Here, tuck in these quilts and furs to soften the boards. And that cloth, too, might as well use it."

They stared into the wagon bed but didn't make a move to climb in. I arranged the quilts and such as cozy as I could.

"Miss Delight, do you think you might ride with me in the wagon?"

She nodded. "One old woman not worth much worry. Somebody sees us, you say I'm a healer on my way to a birthin'. Besides, I can't ride under no boards. I get all crawly. But you boys, climb in now."

We settled them in and tucked quilts around them. I tried to talk real serious, but kindly like Papa. "Now, fellas, once we start, you can't make noise or move around. It's dangerous; you've got to lie still and stay real quiet. If you can sleep, that's best. Understand?"

They nodded and looked solemn. Miss Delight repeated my warnings and added her own, complete with prayers and scoldings.

One spoke. "You going to lay them boards down tight? Like a coffin?"

Dear Lord, what could I say to that? "It ain't a coffin, more like a bed with sides. But I'll tell you something. My sister once rode in a real coffin for days and days. She lived to tell about it and so will you."

I set the boards back in place gently, hiding six frightened faces. Miss Delight helped haul our goods and food back into place on top.

As I buckled harness, Sam nickered. I sighed, wishing we could go hunt for Susannah, but Miss Delight was right; we had to take the fellas north right away.

Charlie tossed his head, and I swung up to the wagon seat. Either God was talking to me or the horses were, but either way, we had to get moving. "Watch over Susannah, Lord. Keep her safe."

"Susa and James," Miss Delight said. "Amen."

"Gee up."

My team began to pick their way back to the road, but I drove with my heart heavy and my ears wide open, straining for the slightest sound. I didn't have much hope that

159

Susannah would meet up with us on this road, but the thought of not finding her at all chewed at me. By taking too long to get south, I'd failed James. Now I'd failed Susannah by not dragging her out as soon as I arrived. Blast!

At the end of the track we turned onto the main road. It started in raining, a good solid rain that might last all day.

Behind me Miss Delight was nodding off. I wanted to wake her and ask if I was doing right—seven people safe and only one missing—but she was old and needed her sleep, so I drove on with only the patter of rain and the morning calls of birds to keep me company.

The sky stayed dreary, and I was glad we traveled the main road, for that rough track would have turned into a swamp. But I stopped feeling glad after about two miles when horses sounded in the distance.

Dang it! I couldn't pull off to hide, for if I could hear their horses, whoever was coming could hear mine. I'd have to hope the folks weren't too nosy. "Miss Delight. Wagon coming. Get ready to be a midwife if anybody sees you."

The road wasn't wide enough for two big haulers, so as the hay wagon approached, I steered to the right to get out of the way. As he passed me, the farmer nodded. "Howdy, stranger. Some rain we got today, hey? What you doin' in these parts?"

"Howdy to you." I lifted my hat with a shaking hand. "I'm a peddler. Been selling cloth and trinkets back in the hills."

"Got anything I might need?" He pulled his horses to stop.

"Sorry. Wagon's near emptied out and I'm bound north to restock. If you tell me the whereabouts of your farm, I'll visit on my next trip." I clenched my fingers into a fist. *Please, please believe me.*

"I live up by the Winchester Road. Gray house, pair of red barns, name's Thompson."

"I'll surely look for your place next time," I offered, knowing full well there'd never be a next time for me in this part of Kentucky.

"Good day to you, then," he said at last. "Godspeed."

After his wagon rolled past, I reclaimed the road and called to my team. "Gee up, boys. Miss Delight, you can rest easy now. Man's gone."

It took a mile of riding before my heart returned to normal speed. We met three such wagons that day. Every time I feared it was Old Josiah Whitely and was relieved when it was only strangers too busy ducking raindrops to bother with me. Still, when the light finally faded and the sky took on the gloomy gray of a damp twilight, I breathed easier.

Along this busy road, Mister Ezekiel had mapped out clearings for us that were well hidden, which meant I nearly missed the one I'd been heading for. But I did find it, dim light and all, for the turning was marked by a tall pine tree struck by lightning and scorched.

When we reached a grassy place hidden by thick

woods, Miss Delight and I shoved my goods to one side and opened up the floorboards to let the fellas climb out.

"Did you ride all right?" I asked. "Did you sleep? Was it bumpy?"

"Couldn't sleep," the littlest one said. "I was too scairt."

"Lemuel kick," said another. "Ain't lying next to him again."

"I sleep just fine," the biggest fella bragged.

"And you snore!" another told him. "Real loud."

We all laughed, and for the first time since this started, I felt like a regular human being instead of a wicked ogre.

"All right," I said. "You can sleep tonight. We'll stay here. No loud noises, nor a fire to draw attention to ourselves, but for now, why don't you run about some, you've been cooped up all day."

Run they did, like when teacher would call recess and we'd bolt from the schoolhouse and race to the meadow. Rain didn't stop those fellas a bit.

Miss Delight watched over them while I unhitched; then I watched over them while she got out our supper, cold beans. The fellas didn't seem to mind the food—after the long day's ride they were plenty hungry. But my mind was so full of plans and worries, I could only eat half my meal.

"We're getting close to the river," I said as they ate. "So listen and remember. If anything goes wrong, you'll still get north safely."

Every fella looked at me then with dark, serious eyes.

"First, you gonna have to know where north be," Miss

Delight began. "Come a clear night, I show you the North Star and the Dipper. They point the way to Canada, to freedom."

"Miss Delight, she's a wise woman," I said. "She'll watch over you. Place you're going to is Windsor, Canada West." I explained again, about the Railroad and how lots of Ohio folks would help them for a night or two after I dropped them off in Ripley. How I'd keep traveling on to Cincinnati so if anybody was following me, they'd be following a false trail—they'd only find a peddler and an empty wagon, not a string of fellas making free. Then I made them repeat the town so they'd get to the right place in case somehow they got separated.

"Remember, now, in Ripley there's a house on the hill over the river."

"How we know which house?" one fella asked.

Miss Delight answered. "Big pile of steps from the river to the top. Candle in the window. One candle say safe to cross. Two say trouble."

They nodded, silent and serious.

"I'll take you to Ripley," I repeated. "Then I'll head back to Cincinnati, where I started. That way, anybody finds me, they won't find you."

The fellas didn't look too pleased, but Miss Delight and I had decided it was safest. If anybody was looking, they'd come after me and my wagon, so we'd split up and confuse things. It was the best we could do.

The fellas had a lot of questions but they sounded more excited than scared, so I figured they'd hold up all right, especially with Miss Delight for a mother hen. She'd keep them behaving and in good spirits if anybody could.

But my spirits kept sinking. I fretted about Susannah and how we'd find her. Wondered how we'd even know if she'd started to run or gotten caught. I couldn't head back up to Canada without her along, so I decided, right then and there, that once Miss Delight and the fellas were safe on their way north, I'd go back and search for Susannah.

Since the ground was wet, we bedded down under the wagon's canvas cover for the night. We packed in pretty tight, but that kept the chill off. When I whispered my plan to go back for Susannah to Miss Delight, she scolded me.

"Ssst. What's wrong with you, William? You got no faith? God won't let us down. Didn't God send all this rain to cover up her scent while she run? Susa gonna come. I feel it."

"Wish I did," I grumbled. "Wish I could see her right now."

"Wishing, huh. Tell you something, young man, sleep'll do you a whole lot more good than wishing. Now, you just shut your eyes and let God take care His business. You helping Him, but you ain't Him." And with that she rolled over and left me alone with my worries.

Chapter 26

Best I could guess, we had a day's ride to the river and Ripley. With that in mind, I shook myself awake when the first birds started singing the next morning, and we were packed and on the road before full light. The rain had slowed some, but it still came down, making everything look grim and gloomy. My spirits started to rise, though, for if it kept raining, our trail would wash out, and every mile we covered brought us closer to free soil.

I rode quiet that day, watching for other travelers and for ruts in the road. The mud was getting plenty sticky with all the rain, and I couldn't afford a stuck wheel.

Miss Delight tucked herself into a corner of the wagon where she could sleep. For an old woman, she was making this rough trip better than I'd expected, but with all the sewing and cooking and watching over the fellas, her strength was wearing down, and we still had the river to cross, so I wanted her to rest.

I'd probably never spent so much time alone in my life as I had since leaving Atwater. I enjoyed most of it, for I could do as I liked and nobody bossed or bothered me, or said I'd messed up, or had a better idea.

But a fella could go on too long by himself, and without letters or news, home could feel a million miles away, so I made up letters in my head, letters I'd write as soon as we were all out of danger.

Dear Mama and Papa,
  You won't believe what I've been up to down in Kentucky. . . .

Dear Lucy,
  Get ready, I'm coming up to see you soon. . . .

Dear Elise,
  After you have supper with me, will you walk out and show me the sights in Cincinnati? . . .

Dear Susannah,
  Where are you? Are you coming? Are you safe?

Thinking about Susannah made me worry again, for if I was cold and wet, she'd be feeling worse. I had a wagon;

she'd be on foot. I had folks with me, even if they were asleep or hidden; she had only herself. And I had my horses, the best friends a fella could have on a trip like this one.

"Hey, Charlie. Gee up, Sam. You're doing a good job with all this rain. You've been pulling smooth and steady. Tell you what, when we get ourselves to Cincinnati, I'll treat you real nice. Buy you some apples, some carrots, extra oats. Yes, sir, I'm gonna give you a feast."

Noontime came and went and I ate cold, dry corn bread. Partway through the afternoon, Miss Delight woke up and hummed tunes softly.

"Thank you," I said, looking over my shoulder. "That singing helps."

"Helps me, too, William. Keeps my faith strong. You call out now, if somebody come and should I get quiet again."

But God smiled on us that afternoon and we didn't pass a soul. Even the settlements and farms we drove by were quiet. Every sensible person had probably decided to stay indoors and wait for better weather. So Miss Delight hummed, I drove, and the horses plodded north through gray, shadowy woods.

Daylight was fading when I caught the heavy smell of the river. I urged the horses on, and a quarter hour later there she was, the Ohio, brown and muddy and full of water—the most beautiful sight I ever laid eyes on.

Dark shapes clustered on the opposite shore downstream, the town of Ripley, just where Ezekiel had drawn it. I jumped down to lead my team along the bank.

"Good work, Charlie. Fine job, Sam. You did your part. I'm mighty proud of you both. Soon as we find ourselves a hiding place for this wagon, you'll get your suppers."

The rain finally quit, but a soft mist came off the water like smoke. That mist would hide us as long as we stayed low. Above the mist, houses perched on the banks. We were still upstream from the town. I looked higher. Sure enough, just back from the river, the hillside grew steep. And there, at the top, I saw the light of a single candle. Safe to cross. Thank the Lord.

After the fellas were sprung loose from hiding we secured the horses and wagon in a sheltered place right on the riverbank, where trees overhung, for even in dim light the canvas shone too bright to leave in the open. We packed away all our gear, then pulled out rope and empty barrels.

"How we get across?" asked the little one who couldn't swim.

"Can any of you fellas swim? Stand over here if you can."

Four fellas stepped closer to me. One stayed put, and the little one grabbed on to Miss Delight.

"Good. That helps. Each of you gets a barrel. Put your clothes inside and tap the lid down real tight. Tie a rope on each barrel. Tie the other end around your belly. You that can swim, go right across. If you get tired, haul up your barrel and hold on. Use your legs and kick the rest of the way. Can you do that?"

They nodded.

"Keep together best you can. I don't want to lose anybody in this fog."

They huddled close and fumbled with ropes and barrels.

"All right, you two that can't swim. I'm big and I'm strong. I'll tow you across safe. You get a barrel, and if you kick, it'll help. Now, Miss Delight, you and one fella need to wait on this side till I can make a second trip. You understand?"

"Uh-huh." They both nodded, but the littlest one hung back and grabbed Miss Delight's arm even tighter.

"That's right," she told him. "You and me watch first time."

I bent to test the water. Cool but not cold. We stripped down to our underdrawers and packed the fellas' dry clothes in the barrels. As we waded in, the rocky river bottom poked at our feet. I walked next to the bigger of the fellas who couldn't swim. He and I held tight to the barrel ropes while the swimmers went ahead.

As we waded, the bottom grew rockier and the river rose to our waists, but it didn't get deep. When we'd covered a quarter of the distance, the water just came to my chest. Couple of the fellas, though, they started in swimming, for they were smaller. Then, in a single step, the river bottom fell away, and we all paddled and splashed and kicked.

Two of the swimmers struck off and swam real smooth, disappearing into the wispy fog. The other two swam slow, and pretty soon they grabbed barrels and held on.

169

"You all right?" I called.

"Just got scairt a minute," one said.

"I can kick. I got good legs," the other called.

I treaded water and watched. They weren't ducks, but they seemed strong enough. Putting the rope between my teeth, I began to stroke, slow and steady, keeping the swimmers in front of me as I towed my passenger on the barrel.

We made halfway, then three-quarters. Without warning, my feet struck rock again. I squinted up at the hillside as we waded to shore. We'd drifted past the house with the candle, but not too far.

The night air raised gooseflesh on my skin. We reached the bank and the four swimmers joined up with us. "This here's Ohio," I said. "Free soil. Hallelujah!"

The fellas put on their clothes and set the barrels adrift on the river so nobody would find them and get curious. I searched out the path for the Freedom Steps with the fellas hurrying behind me. Once we spotted the steps, they scampered up like squirrels, and I felt loose, like somebody had just untied a thick rope from around my chest. Five on their way to safety. Two more to go.

I hurried back to the water, waded in again, and had to fight the urge to race across. Durned rain had filled up the river, so I needed to hang on to my strength for the next crossing. On the Kentucky side ghost buildings loomed ahead, farms, most likely. When I could stand, I stayed in chest-high water, hidden by the fog, and battled the

170

current upstream until I'd left the farms behind. Only then could I head for the bank and walk in the shallows.

Miss Delight was watching for me. She'd gotten herself and the little one undressed and she'd calmed him down, so he seemed to think riding a barrel was like having his own boat.

"You can swim, ma'am?"

"Enough," she said. "Let's go."

"But Susannah," I said.

Miss Delight just shook her head and stepped into the water.

The swimming went slower this time, for the river had stolen my strength and Miss Delight was timid in the water. I'd have to make one more trip back for my wagon and team, so I saved my energy. At long last we made a safe passage, and the single candle still burned. Hallelujah again! We pulled the clothes free of the barrels, and I led the old woman and the young fella to the Freedom Steps.

"Remember. Windsor, Canada West."

Miss Delight nodded. She stepped toward me and slipped the leather thong with Noah's arrowhead from around her neck and placed it around mine. "God bless you, William," she said, then, taking the small fella's hand, began to climb the long stairs.

Swallowing hard, I spoke softly, more to myself than to the old woman. "I'm going back for Susannah. You can't stop me." I stood on the riverbank, staring at the misty water, trying to gather my strength to swim back over for the wagon. A small scraping sounded behind me, then a voice.

"Who you talking to, peddler boy? Me or yourself?"

"Susannah?" I spun around and nearly crashed into her. "When? How?" My heart thumped so fast, I couldn't spit out more than a single word at a time.

"Been waiting for you since yesterday," she whispered, pointing up the long dark flight of steps. "They hide me away till the younguns come."

"You got away safe, then. Thank heavens. I've been worrying. Did you see Miss Delight, too?"

"She come up the steps as I come down. We talk a little."

I thought hard, trying to make sense of it all. My job with these folks was done, except for laying the false trail to Cincinnati with my wagon and team. The time had come for goodbyes. "Good luck to you, then, Susannah. I'll head up to Canada one of these days for a visit, so I'll surely see you."

"I ain't going," she said. "A bad feeling sitting right next to my heart. Somebody after us. I ain't leaving you alone to catch trouble."

"Susannah! You're on free soil now. You can't go back south. You've got to go north, to Noah. I'll stay in Kentucky and cross down by Cincinnati. You can't risk that."

"You can't stop me. Anybody come, it be me they be hunting or Miss Delight and them boys. Can't let you face that without help."

"Durn and blast! If they catch me without the fellas, it's bad. A big fine, jail maybe. But if they catch you . . ." I loosed the ropes and set the last two barrels afloat on the river. "Are you a fool?"

She crossed her arms over her chest. "I got this feeling."

"What about the old woman? She needs you."

"We talk before she leave the cabins. She say I can do what I want."

"Then she's a durn fool too!" I growled.

Susannah glared at me and planted her hands on her hips. "Don't you say that about my grand!"

"Your grand? Miss Delight—is your grandmama? Of course she is! Then you've got to go with her!" Blast it!

"She keep care of those boys so they don't mischief and get found. I stick to you till we be out of danger. Now, can we cross over and get them horses moving before morning?"

If she'd have been a fella, I'd have pounded on her, hauled her up the steps. But she wasn't, and besides, she was near as tall as me.

"Durn and blast!" I strode into the water.

Susannah stripped down to her underclothes and followed me into the river, matching me stride for stride, stroke for stroke. A quarter across, then halfway. We were right there, in the deepest, fastest water, when I heard a shout.

"Found it!" a man's voice called out. Hounds bayed.

"Susannah! Tread water." Turning to follow the

173

sounds, I pumped my legs and heard the frightened cries of horses. Charlie! Sam!

I began stroking again, hard, but a hand clamped down on my shoulder.

"Don't!" Susannah said. "Look!"

Along the bank—upstream where I'd left my team and the wagon—a light glowed. A soft haze, small and dim at first, and then bright as the sun.

Somebody had followed us, and they'd set my wagon on fire!

Chapter 27

I dove under the water and stroked toward the burning wagon. Susannah grabbed my foot and yanked on it. When I came up for air, she let go of my foot and latched on to my arm instead. "Shhh," she warned. "What you doing?"

"My horses!" I tried to free my arm, but she held on too tight. "Let go. I can't let Charlie and Sam get burned."

"Ain't nobody gonna burn horses. Where I come from, they treat horses better than folks. William, we got to swim."

I thrashed and fought, but she clung to my arm. "I can't leave my horses."

"You got to. He'll take good care of them."

"But he's burned my wagon. Stolen my horses. My property."

"Ain't I someone's property? Ain't you stealing me? Come on. Swim."

She dragged me westward, and I floated alongside for a moment as her words made their way into my mind. I was stealing her. So it was a trade. But Charlie. Sam. I'd never see my team again.

The hounds bayed and I heard a loud boom, then another. Too loud for rifles, it sounded like a cannon.

I turned.

Flames shot sky-high. Had to be that durned moonshine whiskey. The barrels had blown up and the whiskey was burning too. Blast it!

I stroked westward, and north, toward the Ohio shore. "Let's get to the bank. We can run faster than we can swim."

"No." Susannah spoke softly, but she headed toward the middle of the river. "We got to swim."

"Come on. This fog is thick as cotton. It will hide us."

"Not from noses. Them dogs smell us if we touch the shore. Swim, and quiet."

"We'll make for Ripley," I said. "The Freedom Steps."

She shook her head. "No. The dogs. They'll follow."

I scanned the hilltop. We'd gone a ways past the steps, and as I looked up I caught a glimmer of light at a window, but as I watched, a second candle began to glow out in warning.

Susannah was right. We couldn't go there. The people in that house would have enough to do hiding Miss Delight and the fellas. Our only hope was to stay in the water until we were far away from Ripley. If the men who were chasing us tried to follow Miss Delight and the fellas, it might just give us the time we needed.

I sent up a quick prayer that they would follow Miss Delight. Then I sent up another that the conductor's luck would hold and he'd get her and the fellas out to safe hiding places in time.

Susannah and I swam hard, and with the river's help we rounded one shadowy bend and then another. We approached a town on the Kentucky side and then passed it by. My breath came in short bursts and my lungs burned at every one. If I felt this bad, she must too. "You want to rest. Float some?"

"Yes."

We rolled over onto our backs and drifted for a spell, without words. It felt like floating in a cloud. When I'd caught my breath, I whispered to her, "Sure wish we'd kept the barrels and that rope. We could have made us a fine raft. Let's look for the barrels."

"Too foggy," she said. "But too foggy for catchers to see us, if they looking. How far to this Cincinnati of yours?"

"Cincinnati? It's got to be at least fifty miles! That's two or three days by wagon."

"Better swim again," she said.

I stroked, counting a slow rhythm in my head, and

wondered if we really had to go all the way to Cincinnati. If a person could manage to swim fifty miles, the good Lord only knew how long it would take.

We went on like that for the rest of the night. We swam until our lungs and our muscles burned, then floated with the current to rest. Our spells of swimming grew shorter and our rests grew longer until the sky grayed, the mist thinned, and trees appeared on the riverbanks.

"We've got to hide. We can't swim in daylight, or they'll catch us for sure," I said. "I need a rest. My arms are all used up."

"Mine too." Susannah's voice trembled; it scared me.

"Let's wade awhile. We'll find a place." I led her toward the Ohio side. If someone saw us, at least we'd have a chance. Not every Ohio person obeyed that blasted Fugitive Slave Act and returned a runaway to the owner.

We trudged along, knee-deep and shivering, watching both banks. No towns, nor people to see us yet. The sky went from dark gray to light gray, then pink. Full day was coming, and the sun would soon burn off the mist. Every minute we stayed in the river, the risks worsened. We couldn't go south to Kentucky. But Ohio was only a little safer these days; slave catchers patrolled the riverbanks.

The sun broke behind us as we rounded a bend in the river, and I saw a dark shape up ahead. Land, with willow trees and water on both sides. An island.

"Get down in the water. I'll swim out to that island

and snoop around. If it's empty, I'll whistle once. If it's got houses or people, I'll whistle twice and you sneak past, real quiet."

Susannah nodded and knelt in the water so only her nose and the top of her head showed.

I dug for the last of my strength and made for the island. Once I felt pebbles under my feet, I wanted to sink down and sleep, but Susannah waited all alone in the river, so I walked up one side and down the other. The island wasn't too big, an acre or two at most. Long and skinny, with two forks at one end and a hooked spit of land at the other. And, hallelujah, not a soul on the place but me.

I whistled once. Susannah swam in slow, tired strokes. When she made the island, I helped her climb over a pile of sharp rocks. My arms and legs shook with cold and exhaustion. Hers did too.

"Where . . . Where we be?"

"I don't know. But it's quiet. Looks safe. We can sleep here, swim again tonight. There's a place where the grass grows high. Might be soft ground there. Come on."

She followed without complaint, and when we got to the tall grass, we both just fell into it. Soft ground or lumpy, I sure didn't notice, for I sank deep into sleep.

Chapter 28

A whistle blast jolted me awake. The sun was high, grass brushed my face, and I sat up, confused. Felt like I was in the hay meadow where Tom and I sunned ourselves after a dip in the creek. But what was that terrible noise?

I looked around and spied a flatboat drifting down the river. The Ohio! Long way from Atwater and our farm. As the night's events rushed back into my mind, I looked around. Susannah had heard the noise too, for she sat up, careful as a cat.

I crept through the grass to sit next to her and whispered, "Are you all right? Did you sleep enough?"

"I'll do," she said. "Where we be? How far we come?"

She crossed her arms over her chest to cover herself. She wore rough underclothing, but it only covered her from shoulder to knee.

I glanced down at myself, wearing only a pair of underdrawers, and felt my face heat up. I hoped she wouldn't look at me too close, for there was more skin than cloth showing. "Don't know. Never rode the river before. I'm starved."

She nodded. "Last meal, those Quaker folks fed me, last night."

At her words my stomach growled. We'd worked plenty hard with all the swimming. Then it hit me. Everything was gone. Stolen or burned. All we had was ourselves and the skimpy clothing we wore.

"Oh, blast it! Charlie . . . Sam . . ."

"Shhh. I know. They bad men who come after me."

"It's not your fault. If I'd been smarter . . ."

"Do you think my grand . . ." She sniffed. "Do you think she and them boys made it safe?"

I reached for a smile to reassure her. "From what I've heard, the man at the Freedom Steps, he's got lots of fine people working with him. Never lost a soul. They'll be fine. It's us I'm worried about. We're barely covered, we've got no food. And I don't know how far it is to Cincinnati."

"I ain't come all this way just to give up." She glared at me and I couldn't help but admire her. She'd walked alone to free soil and swum the river all night. Somehow, I'd have to get us on the right road again.

"We need to eat. If we get food, can you swim again tonight?

"Sure, long as this old river help us."

I reached around my waist for my money belt. Oh, no!

"Durn and blast! I left my money with my clothes and boots—didn't want the coins to weigh me down, Susannah. What a dolt I am! You still got that money I gave you?"

She chewed her lip. "Two dolts," she said. "I give it to my grand; I figure you got enough. Oh, Will! I'm sorry!"

"Well, we won't eat real soon unless we can find some roots or berries. Let's look."

We scoured the island and found one small patch of blackberries and a bunch of greens Susannah said we could eat. Between us we made quick work of that, and, if anything, it only made my stomach feel emptier.

"I worked for meals before," I said. "I could swim across to the Ohio side, put in a day's labor, and get paid in food."

She shook her head. "Dress like that? Best not. I might catch us a fish."

My cheeks burned again. "We got no fire to cook it on and no way to start one, even if we dared the smoke."

When I said that word, *smoke*, it reminded me of the night before and all the sounds and smells—the horses' frightened cries, the hounds, the explosion.

"Those catchers. They won't give up." I closed my eyes and could see that durned wall of runaway notices. In a day or two Susannah's name, Miss Delight's, the fellas', even mine would get pasted up there with big rewards offered. I shuddered at the thought: We weren't safe anywhere but Canada.

"We got to keep hiding, then," she said. "With my dark skin and your red hair, we can't get seen in daylight."

"Wish we had a boat." I sighed.

"We got strong arms. Strong hearts. I ain't giving up!"

"Course not. And I won't let you down. We've got the river to drink, so we won't die. We can go hungry for a day or two. Can't be that far to Cincinnati. How about we sleep again, so when night comes we'll be ready to swim?"

"All right."

We crept back to the tall grass and stretched out. After a time, I heard her breathing get real regular, so I knew she slept, but I couldn't. Thoughts of Charlie and Sam, the money, and everything I'd lost crowded in.

I remembered the Bible Mama and Papa had given me to bless my trip, and all those letters I'd tucked into its pages. Ashes now. Or were they? What if the men after us had searched my wagon first, stolen my money, read the letters? That could get Mama and Papa in trouble. And Elise! I didn't know which was worse, burned-up letters or stolen ones. I'd never see them again in either case.

And what might happen next? Even if I could get us to Cincinnati, we'd need clothes. I'd have to steal from some farm wife's clothesline. A bad thing, but I couldn't parade down the streets of Cincinnati in my drawers.

Supposing we got that far, found clothes and all, we could either head for Walnut Hills and the Quakers or ask Elise for help. That shop was a lot closer to the river, which meant less chances to get caught. But I worried about what Elise would think of me, and what her mother might do, strict as she was. It didn't bear fretting about.

Susannah slept the afternoon away while I worried, planned, slapped at mosquitoes, and counted the boats that passed. I heard dogs barking, too, and prayed they were just farm dogs, not hounds on our trail. Rain clouds gathered and the sky darkened. I nudged her awake. "You remember where we're going?" I asked.

"Sure. Windsor, Canada West. Find Noah."

"Yep, but first we've got to get to Cincinnati. I have friends there and you need to remember their names, so if something else bad happens, you can get help."

"What bad things?"

I shrugged. "I don't know. I just want to be ready. Listen, there's a girl—Elise—her mama runs a dress shop. Schmidt's Fine Ladies' Mercantile. It's on Market Street in the town, not far from the river. You got that?"

She nodded. "Schmidt's Fine Ladies'. Market Street. Elise. What else?"

"North of town, there's a place. Walnut Hills. It's a pretty village with lots of walnut trees. You know what walnuts look like?

"Yes."

"Quaker folk live there. Look for men with big round hats and plain dark clothes. They can help you."

"Why you say all this, William?"

The first raindrops spattered my arm. "Just to be safe. Anything could happen. Dogs, men with horses, boats, anything. Remember, if trouble comes, go to Elise or the Quakers."

"All right. You think it got dark enough to swim?"

"Might as well start. Cincinnati's still a long way."

The water was cold again and my arms began to ache, but I tried for an even pace and blessed the current that helped carry us west.

As we swam I watched the shoreline. Josiah Whitely and John Merrick would surely hunt for us with men and dogs. The danger was great and only the river was our friend.

But even that friend let us down. We'd been on the water for maybe three hours and were resting, floating on our backs.

"You feel that, William? We going faster?"

Once she mentioned it, I paid attention. Sure enough, the current had picked up. "River's faster, louder too. Guess it wants to ride us to old Cincinnati in style. I ain't complaining."

In spite of being hungry and tired, it felt fine to bob down that river fast, like some old-time birch bark canoe. I lay back and enjoyed it until I felt myself being tugged toward the Ohio shore. Was a rapids coming? A falls?

185

"Susannah! Look out! Swim for Kentucky, quick!"

Before I could say durn and blast, boiling water surrounded me. I raised my head but couldn't see much, just what looked like another river, roaring out to join the Ohio.

Currents and eddies tugged and spun me around. I stroked hard for the Kentucky shore, but that seemed to make the river angry—it whirled me faster. Rushing water spun me and robbed me of breath, leaving me no time to feel scared.

Then the river dragged me under and tumbled me in circles. I stroked hard, but my arms gave out. When I opened my mouth to yell, water rushed in, and without giving me even a minute to breathe, the river hurled me deep. I felt a thud, felt myself smashing into something hard. Then blackness came down, cold and wet and brutal blackness.

Chapter 29

When I came to, every part of me ached. I tried to stretch my arms, but they seemed stuck and I was still moving. "Susannah?" It came out like a croak.

She tugged on my shoulder. "William? You waking up?"

"Ooo. What happened? My arms . . ." It felt like I was trussed up, tied to something. And my leg!

She pulled on me some more until she'd hauled me close to the riverbank and I could sit. My head pounded.

"What did you do to my arms?"

"Found a tree limb. Tore off a strip of my shift and tied you to the limb. Had to keep your face out the water."

"But what happened?"

"You call out. I get away. You spin and spin. That river, he spit you out, then smack you hard, right into something. Old dead tree most likely. But you breathing and moaning, so I know you ain't dead, just poorly."

"Sounds like a whirlpool. I thought I saw another river dumping into the Ohio."

"River carry us," she said. "I grab hold so you don't drift away."

"But my leg?"

"Old river, he break it for you. I been pulling you down to that Cincinnati. Maybe you get it fixed there. Can you keep going?"

"I can try. My head. My leg . . ." I faded again.

That happened on and off all night. I'd wake up for a while, feel myself being towed down the river, then slip back under a cloud, where it didn't hurt so much.

Finally the moving stopped and a breeze tickled my skin. I opened my eyes. The sun wasn't up yet, but the sky was pale. "Where are we?"

"Big town. Hope this be your Cincinnati. I can't go no farther." Susannah was working at knotted strips of cloth that bound my arms to a branch. I sat on the ground with my left leg stuck out in front of me. It hurt like sin.

When I turned my head to see where we were, a wave of dizziness came and went, but at least I knew. "Cincinnati. Do you think . . . Can you get me to that shop?"

She wrestled my arms free and I stretched them. They were sore as the dickens, but they worked.

"Hold on to me," she said. "See if you can stand." She

pulled on my arms. After several tries I got to my feet, but once up, I swayed and nearly tumbled down again.

"You won't make no shop," she said. "Here. Let's get you over between those buildings where nobody can see you."

She half dragged me across a dock and into an alley. I slid to the ground again, hoping nobody would pass by and see me in just my drawers. My left leg was on fire. "The shop . . . three streets that way, then turn left at a tavern. Two more streets. Look for fancy ladies' clothes." I pointed, but the dizziness buzzed around me again.

"You hold on, William. I be back."

I don't know how long I waited there. Every once in a while I opened my eyes, but everything looked wavy, and I couldn't tell if the sky was getting lighter or if it was just my head that wasn't working right. Finally a cart rattled and voices came near.

"*Ja*, that's him all right. Quick, get him in the cart and cover him up."

Strong arms tugged and lifted me. A blanket dropped down over me and surrounded me with warm darkness. I felt a thump and heard wheels squeak and went under again. Then all the movement stopped.

"*Ja*. Go for the doctor, Elise."

I opened my eyes and moaned. Daylight. A woman bending over me. Everything looked fuzzy.

"Shhh. The doctor, he comes soon. We get you into bed now."

More tugging and pulling.

I looked around. A room came into focus. Elise's mama. "Mrs. Schmidt?" I croaked. "Elise? Susannah?" Those few words tired me out. My left leg throbbed, and my head felt like somebody was pounding on it with a big rock.

"*Ja.* You got to Cincinnati with Gott's help. You ver lucky ve vere still here. Two more nights and ve'll be gone."

Gone? I couldn't imagine what she was talking about, and my head hurt too bad for me to try and figure it out, so I let go and dozed.

When I woke again everything still hurt, but I felt safe, taken care of by Elise's mama. I opened my eyes. People bustled around like they were having a party. When I tried to sit up, the room swirled, so I sank back into the pillow.

A man with a German accent poked me and peered into my eyes. "*Ja,* he'll mend. Young man, I strapped up your leg real tight. It broke in two places. You keep still and don't try to walk soon, you'll mend. All the rest is just cuts and bruises."

"I broke my leg in two places?" My voice sounded strange in my ears, more like a duck than me.

"*Ja.* You got caught in a big virlpool. Vere the Little Miami Creek joins the Ohio. Only it isn't so little ven ve've had such rains. Rough water, sure enough."

"It spun me around and around." I closed my eyes and remembered the tug of water on my body and the blackness that came down.

"Und I suppose you fought the current?"

Had I fought the river? I thought for a moment, tried to make my mind work. "Yes, sir. Gave it my all, sir. Swam as hard as I could."

"*Ja*. Vell, sometimes a person has to let the river decide. Let the current carry you und vait for the right moment to svim free. But you vill not be svimming again for some time now, Villiam."

"No, sir. I won't."

As strong and foreign as the doctor's accent sounded, he reminded me of Papa. Papa had always given me the same sort of advice. "Don't fight everything, Will. Don't always swim upstream. Choose your moments carefully." Tarnation.

"Susannah?"

"I'm fine, William."

I relaxed at the sound of her voice. "How did you . . . ?"

"Hush now. We tell you everything when the doctor get done."

"Feed him soup," the doctor instructed. "Bread this evening. And tomorrow, more soup, more bread. Drops of laudanum for the pain if he needs, but only to sleep. I'll come back afternoons."

Mrs. Schmidt propped me up in the bed. I could sit this time without dizziness. My left leg lay on a fat pillow, strapped to a board. It still throbbed, and my stomach was empty and growling.

Elise brought soup and a spoon. Her mama sat next to me and began to feed me like I was some overgrown baby, but I was too starving and tired to argue.

"Tell me," I said between hot, rich-tasting spoonfuls.

"She was so brave. She came here at daybreak and took us to you," Elise said. "You were soaking wet and bleeding and your leg was bent all crooked."

"How did you manage?" I asked Susannah.

"Susannah was wonderful," Elise interrupted. "Took the three of us to haul you back here, Will. You sure are big."

"You know about . . . Susannah? She's running . . ."

Elise's mama nodded. "*Ja*. She tell us everything. The young boys, the old voman, the steps, everything. You are a brave boy, Villiam. But you took terrible chances."

"You won't tell?" I squinted at Mrs. Schmidt.

She didn't smile. "I come to this country to make a life. Vould I send anybody to a bad place? I vould not. I could not."

Things faded again. I'd sleep, wake up and eat, get a few questions answered, and then sleep again. Toward the end of the second day, the doctor came back and said I could travel next morning if I kept my leg strapped and packed it in with quilts and pillows so the wagon ride wouldn't jar it.

I wasn't sure why we had to travel. At first I figured it was Susannah—Mrs. Schmidt and Elise would get her started toward Canada. But by the time they hoisted me up to the wagon, I knew it was more complicated. Household goods surrounded me. Susannah rode hidden behind a pile of ladies' merchandise.

Best I could piece it together, something bad had

happened with the bank and Elise's uncle after the river flooded. They'd lost their shop and were heading north, to find a new home. They'd decided to try Columbus, but if that didn't suit, they'd go all the way to Cleveland.

Now, that was a real piece of luck, for with a busted leg and no wagon or horses, I'd been worrying and stewing about how to get Susannah and myself north. Seemed like in spite of all the trouble, maybe God would keep an eye on us after all.

Epilogue

Oberlin, Ohio
October 1854

So I sit here, hidden away first by Lucy's landlady and then by my sister herself when she returned to the college in September. I scribble, count the days until my leg heals up enough for me to ride again, and wonder if things ever work out the way they're supposed to. When Papa came to see me, he said, "Don't question the wisdom of the Lord."

But still, every time I think about Noah and touch the arrowhead, I wonder at how many ways one fella can go wrong.

I went down to Kentucky to be a peddler and make

money. Well, I failed—lost money, and my horses and wagon.

I intended to steal James away from old John Merrick but failed in that, too. Instead of James, I found six fellas, Susannah, and an old woman, or they found me. But I did get them started on the path to freedom. Miss Delight and the fellas took another three weeks to reach Canada after I left them at the Freedom Steps. Friends helped them every mile along the way.

They're safe now, up in Windsor with Noah, starting a big farm. Lucy met up with them, and from what she says, Susannah and Miss Delight are running things and bossing everybody six ways from Sunday. I've made a promise to them and to myself. Everywhere I go I'll keep looking for James. We're asking people on the Railroad to watch out for him too. I'm not taking off this arrowhead until he gets up to Windsor with Noah and Susannah where he belongs.

Susannah. I was determined to carry that girl across the Ohio River and get her north. Turned out she was the one who carried me and saved my hide doing it. We rode north together, like we were a couple of lacy petticoats, tucked into a wagon filled to overflowing with Elise and her mother's things. What a trip that was. Propped between some big crates, we could barely move. And anytime another wagon appeared, Elise would pile quilts and bonnets on top of us until I was sure I'd suffocate. But we made it.

Elise. That was a big disappointment. I'd planned to

return to Cincinnati all puffed up and proud and treat her to the finest supper a person could find in that town. Instead, I showed up soaking wet, starving hungry, nearly naked, with busted leg. My dreams of a fine supper turned into her mama feeding me beef broth and scolding me.

But the real thing I wanted, I did find. At least I hope so. I've got me a place now. Can't stay in Ohio; they've been looking for me all over—Atwater, Cincinnati, Columbus, Cleveland. With this red hair, a big fella like me can't hide forever.

Next week, I'm cutting my hair real short, hiding the red with bootblack, and heading up to Canada myself. Once we got to talking about it in the wagon, Elise and her mama decided Windsor sounded like a nice enough town. And it didn't have any fancy shops, so it needed at least one.

I'll help out in that shop with the heavy work. And I'll save up and get me a new wagon so I can haul goods to the little villages and farms close by on a regular schedule. We'll be business partners, the Schmidts and me.

At planting time and harvest, I'll work on Susannah's farm. And in winter, when the roads get too full of snow to travel, I'll help Noah take down trees to clear more cropland.

From what Lucy says, and the big old grins she shines around, she and Jeremiah won't be following too far behind me. Lucy's got herself all signed up to teach in the school in Windsor year-round once she finishes college next spring. And the school's big enough that it needs

196

two teachers, so I'll wager her Quaker, Jeremiah Strong, signs up to be the other one.

When Mama and Papa visited, they blessed my plans and my sister's. "Now, son. Don't expect Windsor, Canada, to be heaven on earth," Papa warned. "Folks are folks. Good ones and bad everywhere."

Used to be, I'd have argued with him. Told him I'd find a place that was only good, or else I'd keep looking. But shoot, if I can find a place that's partly good, it's enough for me. I don't expect perfect anymore. Guess I found out I'm not exactly perfect myself.

All I want is a place where they give a fella a chance. To live and breathe free. Make a life, if he's strong enough. So I'm off to Canada in a week. I got lots of friends there, waiting for me to cross the lake, so I'll be fine. And it won't be long till I've earned me a new wagon, with wheels spinning again, maybe not up in the air like in that song, but spinning just the same, on good, solid Canada soil

Yes, sir. You can bet on it.

Author's Note

This is a wet book—it rains and rains and rains. In the days before locks and dams were built, the flow of water in the rivers depended entirely on rainfall and snowmelt. In early spring the water would often rise quickly, causing rivers to overflow their banks and flood. During a long, hot summer dry spell, however, the Ohio could become as shallow as one foot deep. Boat traffic would stop, and a person could wade across with no difficulty. For Will's journey to end with risk and adventure, the river needed to be quite full, so it had to rain a lot.

During the 1800s many Northern boys and men took to the roads and headed south to make their fortunes as peddlers. They braved bad weather, poor roads, and loneliness to bring scarce city goods to isolated farms. Some succeeded and eventually opened stores in the growing towns; others grew tired of endless muddy travel and chose other occupations. Some peddlers specialized in certain goods—such as tinsmiths, who sold, traded, and repaired metal items—but most carried general merchandise.

To the farmers deep in the hills, these shopkeepers on wheels brought not only the physical necessities of life but also news, gossip, sometimes even the mail. And yes, a few Yankee peddlers brought radical ideas and the routes to freedom tucked in between the calicoes and laces.

Free or slave? That was the most divisive question Americans faced in the mid-1800s as the country grew from a few coastal colonies to states that spanned the continent. Every time a new state wanted to join the union, a new political battle was fought, a new compromise hammered out.

Will Spencer's story and his sister Lucy's (told in *North by Night*) both arise as a result of the Fugitive Slave Act, part of the Compromise of 1850. Until that time, while it was possible for a slave owner to follow an escaping slave north and try to recapture him, the Northern (free) states did their best to protect the slaves and limit the rights of such slave owners.

Once the Fugitive Slave Act became the law of the land, a person escaping could be returned to slavery more easily, and even free-born blacks were sometimes captured and forced into slavery if they could be shown to resemble a slave who had escaped. In addition, anyone aiding a runaway could be fined as much as $1,000 and put in jail.

This law incensed Northern abolitionists and stretched the routes on the Underground Railroad tremendously. While before 1850 a slave could travel onto free American soil and cautiously begin a new life, after 1850 the only truly safe destination was Canada. And so communities of former slaves began to develop all along Canada's southern borders.

The rise of cotton also contributed to an increase in runaway slaves and a change in the travelers on the

Underground Railroad. In the early days of slavery most runaways were youngish men, ages eighteen to thirty-five, traveling alone. Once the cotton gin had been invented, however, enormous cotton plantations grew in the Deep South. Huge numbers of people were needed to work the crop, but the importation of new slaves from Africa and from the West Indies had been outlawed in 1808. Where would the cotton workers come from?

In states such as Virginia, Tennessee, Kentucky, and North Carolina, farmers who owned a small amount of land might own a group of ten to fifteen slaves, mostly women. Those slaves would provide labor enough to keep everyone on the farm fed and clothed, and at the same time provide the owner a much-needed source of cash—strong young workers, especially boys, who could be sold south to work the cotton fields.

Once this pattern developed, the breaking up of families to sell young people down the river to the New Orleans slave markets, more and more of the passengers on the Underground Railroad were families—men, women, and children whose only choices were to be forever separated or to run north, to freedom.

Some of those families included pale biracial children, as did some slave families who remained in the South. It wasn't uncommon for a slave owner to be the father of some of his own slaves. Likewise overseers, slave traders, and other men in powerful positions took advantage of slave women and girls themselves, or forced them to have children by men not of their own choosing. For a slave, every choice, every decision, every part of life was owned by another.

As in *North by Night*, Ohio is the starting point for Will's story. In the 1850s it was a state of contrasts, with bustling commercial centers such as Cleveland, Cincinnati, and Columbus, and tiny crossroads farming villages such as Atwater. Its people included settlers from Connecticut whose Northern points of view contrasted with those of settlers from Virginia, who spoke with a Southern accent. Ohio was home to fiery abolitionists and vehement supporters of slavery.

Because of geography, the state provided one of the most direct routes from the slave states to Canada. A person would have to travel approximately 250 miles from the Ohio River crossing to the Great Lakes. Slaves from Kentucky or Virginia (including what is now West Virginia) could travel the moderate terrain in Ohio, compared to the rugged Allegheny Mountains in Pennsylvania.

The times, the places, the frontier spirit, all of these came to life for me as I researched and wrote about the Underground Railroad. On a trip across the country or on a journey through time, it is often hard to understand where we are unless we first understand where we started and how we happened to walk that particular road. I hope you have enjoyed Will's travels and will make many journeys of your own.

Katherine Ayres
Pittsburgh, 2000

201

About the Author

"I discovered the name Delight Webber on a worn tombstone in an old cemetery in Atwater, Ohio," says author Katherine Ayres. "And right away, I began to hear her voice. I knew she'd have an important role in Will's story, but didn't know how important until the writing was under way."

Writing is always a process of discovery for Ayres, who often looks to history for the people and places in her stories. Her previous Delacorte Press books are *Family Tree*, *North by Night: A Story of the Underground Railroad* (a companion to *Stealing South*), and *Silver Dollar Girl*. She also writes History Mysteries for Pleasant Company, as well as plays and poems for children and adults. A founding member of the Playwright's Lab at the Pittsburgh Public Theater, she teaches writing at Chatham College, where she also coordinates the Master of Arts program in children's and adolescent writing.

When she is not writing or researching a book, she skis, golfs, gardens, and quilts. She and her husband live in Pittsburgh and are the parents of three grown children and the grandparents of one little girl.